Symon watched as the a..... ... **propped one hand on her waist impatiently.**

"I stopped by to see Miss B," he said.

"What for?"

"Business."

"Her business is my business right now. I'm her niece."

Niece? Of course. The little girl in fancy dresses whose mother would tug on her arm if she dared even look in the direction of the caretaker's son.

"Is she home?"

"I don't give out information to people I don't know."

Would she, if she knew who he was? "Sorry. Name's Symon Sinclair. I grew up in that cottage down by the creek. I wanted to ask Miss B if I could rent it for a short while."

"I see." The woman's stance relaxed a bit. "Would you like some iced tea?"

"Yes, thank you."

"Just run around to the front porch and I'll bring it out."

He watched her graceful sway as she meandered across the lawn in her bare feet. She glanced over her shoulder and caught him staring.

"Ma'am, I didn't catch your name," he said, as if he didn't know.

"I didn't throw it." She smiled, opened the screen door and disappeared into the house.

YVONNE LEHMAN

is an award-winning bestselling author of fifty books, including mystery, romance, young adult, women's fiction and mainstream historical. She founded the Blue Ridge Mountains Christian Writers Conference and directed it for twenty-five years, and she now directs the Blue Ridge "Autumn in the Mountains" Novel Retreat, held annually at the Ridgecrest/LifeWay Conference Center near Asheville, North Carolina.

YVONNE LEHMAN

The Caretaker's Son

HEARTSONG
PRESENTS

Recycling programs
for this product may
not exist in your area.

™ LOVE INSPIRED BOOKS

ISBN-13: 978-0-373-48654-0

THE CARETAKER'S SON

www.LoveInspiredBooks.com

Printed in U.S.A.

Jesus said...You will know the truth,
and the truth will set you free.
—*John 8:31–32*

To my precious friend and daughter, Cindy Wilson,
who toured Savannah, Georgia, with me
and shares her great insights on my writing ideas.

Chapter 1

A whimper sounded from the back floorboard.

Symon Sinclair shot a glance over his shoulder. "Pipe down now." He returned his attention to steering his black sports car along the streets lined with live oaks and dripping with garlands of Spanish moss. "This is what I came here for."

Hearing the compliant sigh, he continued to reminisce, loud enough for the dictating machine to record his thoughts. Soon, however, his mind moved from childhood to his current surroundings—a city laid out in squares. He was driving along the streets of one of the largest historic districts in the nation, passing churches, mansions, monuments, well-known landmarks and perfectly manicured landscapes.

It had come close to being devastated like Atlanta during the Civil War when General Sherman burned, looted and destroyed. Maybe this city had been too beautiful even for Sherman, who spared it.

The little snatches he knew of Savannah's history intrigued him. He'd need to do research for his project, even though he'd grown up here. Not here, really. He'd been on the outside, looking in. He switched off the recorder he'd dictated into while driving from New York to an overnight stop at a bookstore manager's apartment in Raleigh, and this morning on to Savannah, Georgia. The higher the sun rose in the sky and the closer he got to his exact destination, the more excited and apprehensive he became.

He hadn't seen Miss B in four years. He'd come back two years ago, but that had been to pour his dad's cremated ashes into the creek. He hadn't tried to see Miss B then. She probably hadn't known he was on the property since he had gone to a part of the creek where he wouldn't be visible from the house. Then he'd hightailed it back to New York—on a jet plane.

Turning onto the property, he rolled down the windows and the aroma of growing, blooming foliage assaulted his senses. His eyes couldn't believe the sight of the lush green lawn that looked more like a shag rug than a velvet carpet.

His dad would never have allowed that. To his dad, the lawn had to be perfect. He had believed in and taught Symon the secret of prevention. *Do the job before it's needed,* he'd say, *or you end up with twice the trouble.*

Symon felt a smile form. Miss B had applied that secret to him and his fertile mind. There was no telling what her instruction and nurture had prevented in his life.

He drove past the caretaker's cottage and continued up the long drive to the antebellum mansion with its porch, on which she had cultivated his storytelling ability. His glance lifted to the branches of the huge oaks laden with Spanish moss that formed a canopy overhead.

He needed to tell Miss B what he thought of her. That the lessons had really got through to him. That he had learned which part of his life was the lie and which was the truth.

Like when he was a child, the truth was always the hardest. But he had to face it or end up a pile of alcoholic ashes floating down a creek. And at age twenty-nine, this seemed the time to give it serious thought.

With hardly a glance at the house, he resisted the urge to stop, race up to the front porch and lean against the tall white column and prop a foot on the top step. Oblivious to any changes that might have occurred through the years, he parked in a clearing near the back patio, under an oak bearded with the pale gray fringe of moss. Seeing his traveling mate eager to be released from the confines of the backseat, Symon exited the car and opened the door for Mudd to squeeze out from behind the driver's seat. His companion hesitated, displaying the same kind of misgiving in his eyes that Symon felt.

"Come on, boy. Everything's all right."

The dog apparently believed him and jumped down. He sauntered away with the slight limp of his left back leg.

Symon slammed the car door and strode down the yard, wondering if his eyes deceived him. He stopped in his tracks. Where was the cherry tree? He could not have forgotten where it should be, halfway between the brick patio and the wooded area.

If that doesn't beat all... "Who cut down the cherry tree?"

"I think it's a well-known fact that George Washington did it."

That didn't sound like Miss B. Symon turned quickly, having had no idea anyone was around.

That didn't *look* like Miss B either.

Standing about three feet from him on the wide green croquet lawn was the prettiest just-ripe Georgia peach he'd seen in a long time.

Not only did her soft Southern drawl indicate it, but so did the way she complemented her midthigh white shorts and red T-shirt. Her dark brown hair, golden-touched by the sun, was bound into a thick tress that fell over one shoulder. Her lifted chin and steady gaze made him feel as if she'd caught him with his foot stuck in a picket fence.

That reminded him of Miss B, along with the unusual color of what his dad would have called amethyst eyes. He'd thought that was a cuss word—still wasn't sure he could spell it—until years later he learned it was a color somewhere between blue, purple or violet. He thought hers might be a wee bit lighter than Miss B's. And not at all as inhibiting, despite her apparent efforts.

She was sweet tea and apple pie all rolled up into one, standing there in the warm, humid afternoon.

Amethyst eyes kept gazing at him, waiting for him to comment on George Washington, he reckoned. In New York, he'd *suppose,* but being back in Georgia made him *reckon.*

Forcing his mind from the Georgia peach to the cherry tree stump wasn't the easiest thing to do, but his livelihood depended upon it. He held out his hand to the stump. "This ruins everything."

"Well, it's gone, mister. And I think that might be a good idea for you, too, unless you have a good reason for being here."

Chapter 2

Symon watched as she propped one hand on the waistline of her shorts. The other hand held a cell phone. Those things could be deadly. Her red T-shirt might have taken his mind off the missing tree had it not been the color of cherries.

"I stopped by to see Miss B."

"What for?"

"Business."

"Her business is my business right now. I'm her niece."

Niece? Of course. The baby he hadn't cared about, the toddler who wailed when she didn't get her way and the little girl in fancy dresses, straw hats, black shiny shoes, Shirley Temple ringlets, big blue eyes and her mother's tug on her arm if she dared even look in the direction of the caretaker's son and the darker children of Willamina the cook.

"Is she home?"

"I don't give out personal information to people I don't know."

Would she, if she knew who he was? "Sorry. I forgot

my manners seeing the tree slaughtered nearly to the roots. Name's Symon Sinclair. I grew up in that cottage down by the creek. My dad was Miss B's caretaker."

Her stance switched to at ease, although the color tinting her cheeks indicated otherwise. "Oh. I'm sorry. I heard the sad news."

"Thank you." Did she mean she was sorry he was only the caretaker's son, or sorry about the death of his dad? "I wanted to ask Miss B if I could rent the cottage for a short while if it's not in use."

"Oh, my goodness." Her amethyst eyes widened and she folded her hands, with the cell phone between them. "You're an answer to prayer. This place needs tending. You take care of these grounds and you can stay in the cottage for free. This place has just gone to the dogs."

"Dogs?"

"That's just an expression."

"I know. But it sounds derogatory. Please don't say it around my dog." He tilted his head toward the trees where his dog strolled along the edge.

She tore her gaze from him and looked off across the wavy green lawn to the trees. "That's your…dog?"

"Yes, ma'am."

"What's his name?"

"Mudd."

"Mud?" Her eyes squinted and she rubbed a couple of fingers with her thumb. "You mean, like dirt?"

He heaved a sigh. "Mudd, with two *d*'s to make him feel important. And *you* might call it dirt, but I call mud an adhesive that sticks things together. He and I stick together." She appeared momentarily speechless, and he added, "I could've named him Clay since he's that reddish color, but I prefer Mudd."

He detected a family resemblance in the lift of her eyebrow. "How long have you had him?"

"Just a few months. Since a hurricane left him hurt and homeless."

The eyebrow returned to its appropriate place and a hint of a smile appeared. "That was nice of you."

He gave a half smile and watched Mudd, who kept looking back, afraid to venture off too far.

"Would you like some iced tea? And we can talk about what needs to be done."

Now that sounded like a Miss B request of many years ago. "Yes, thank you."

She turned to go inside and gestured toward the side of the house. "Just run around to the front porch and I'll bring it out."

Would she? Or would she have Willamina do that? Was Willamina still around? He watched her graceful sway as she meandered across the lawn in her bare feet, which sported red-painted toe nails. She glanced over her shoulder and caught him staring.

"Ma'am, I didn't catch your name," he said, as if he didn't know.

"I didn't throw it." She opened the screen door and disappeared into the house.

A mite sassy, that girl.

He stuck his hands into his pants pockets and walked around the house, smiling. Sure was good to be back in the south again. Glancing around, he saw Mudd loping toward him.

Moments later, he sat on the porch and leaned against the column that rose to the second-floor balcony. He propped one foot on the porch with his knee bent and the other on the top step. She came out with two glasses and handed him one. Her ring finger was bare. "Thank you, Miss Annabelle."

She drew a quick breath. "How did you know my name?"

"I…" He started to say *was,* but mentally edited it. "I *am* the caretaker's son." In some circles, once a caretaker's son, always a caretaker's son. "You were four or five years younger than I. Perhaps you don't remember me."

He sipped the tea. Cool, good, sweet.

She didn't respond, but sat in one of the six rocking chairs spread across the wide porch flanked by the white banister. She crossed her ankles.

He supposed that wasn't a good thing to say. Miss Annabelle wasn't supposed to have noticed the caretaker's son.

His quick perusal of the property gave him pause. Why wasn't everything perfect like it had always been? Because his dad was gone? Or had it just seemed perfect when he was younger?

He looked at her again. "Is Miss B all right?"

"Yes, Aunt B's fine. She's visiting a friend at Tybee Island for a few days."

"Ah," he said, remembering. "Miss Clovis?"

At Annabelle's nod and questioning expression he added, "Miss B sometimes took me there when I was just a little tyke. She would show me the turtle eggs. Then, after a few weeks, Miss Clovis would call and say they were beginning to hatch, and she'd take me again."

Annabelle's questioning eyes now held a hint of surprise, but she smiled faintly and her expression softened. "Oh, the Turtle Trot is amazing. Those little hatchlings head across the beach and make their way to the sea."

"Natural instinct," he said, "knowing where their home is."

When his gaze shifted to the cottage, so did hers. That had been his home. He'd tried to make New York his home. Was it natural instinct that had led him back to Savannah?

Or was this a mistake?

He thought Annabelle might ask where his home was when she turned her eyes toward him again, so he quickly said, "I suppose Miss B and Miss Clovis are going to trot in the race."

She almost laughed, but didn't. Instead, she chuffed lightly. "Maybe the walk on the beach. She and Clovis like to be there for the fund-raising kick-off. And then there's the release of the loggerhead sea turtle."

"How long is Miss B staying on Tybee?"

"She doesn't know exactly. She just left yesterday. But it's only twenty minutes away so she can come and go any time. Did she know you were coming?"

No, he hadn't done the polite thing. He had to know first-hand, see it in her eyes, on her face. "Just thought I'd drop in." Rather than explain further, he traveled another route. "Why is it nobody's been taking care of the place, yet some-body cut down the cherry tree?"

Her glance moved toward the lawn and an eyebrow lifted as if she saw nothing amiss. "Aunt B said she didn't want a caretaker living on the grounds. She just calls in someone oc-casionally. But it doesn't look all that bad to me."

No, it didn't look bad. But it wasn't perfect. And he knew the answer. His dad wasn't there. Neither said that.

"Lightning struck the cherry tree," she said. "Then it started rotting away."

A meow drew her out of the rocker and she opened the screen door for a white ball of fluff to stroll out as if she owned the porch. The cat settled herself beside the rocker, to which Miss Annabelle returned, and Annabelle glanced at Miss Independence, who did not glance at Symon.

"SweetiePie," Annabelle said and Symon figured that must be the cat's name but knew you couldn't judge a character, a person or an animal by its name. Mudd knew that, too. The dog slunk back at the corner of the porch and peeked around while SweetiePie-misnomer pretended neither Symon nor Mudd existed.

Seeing that the cat settled like the sweet, docile thing a Persian was noted to be, Mudd ventured close. When he got to midway past the banisters, slowly approaching while the two humans observed, SweetiePie got to her feet. That sweet, calm ball of white fur turned into a snarling, hissing, threatening monster, like a character in one of Symon's thriller novels.

Who would've suspected?

He would.

That was how his mind worked.

Annabelle apparently hadn't expected the cat to act that way, however. She gasped. "SweetiePie, no." She jumped up and grabbed the cat.

Mudd whimpered and his tail retreated between his hind legs.

Annabelle picked up SweetiePie, who became her darling again as if she'd been saved from her worst enemy. But it wasn't Mudd who had threatened her.

Annabelle opened the screen and dropped the cat inside.

Mudd approached warily.

The cat stretched up against the screen.

Opening the screen, Annabelle sweetly shooed the cat away and closed the wood door. "Aunt B's SweetiePie wouldn't hurt a fly," she declared, returning to the rocker. She waved a graceful hand. "Well, maybe a fly or a spider. I guess she's just protecting her territory." Her glance moved from Symon to Mudd and back again.

Yes. He and Mudd were the intruders.

SweetiePie was doing what came naturally, like Annabelle did when she found Symon in the backyard—she got her back up.

Symon drank from the glass and set it on the step below him.

Mudd strolled up to the steps, first eyeing the closed door and then the glass. Symon knew what might happen when Mudd came closer to sniff the glass, but he was careful not to injure his dog's sensitive feelings. SweetiePie had already done that.

Sure enough, his tongue appeared and knocked it over. Symon picked it up and set it on the porch. Mudd licked the tea and started on the ice, playing with it like a cat with a mouse.

Symon looked over at Miss Annabelle wiggling her red toenails while she rocked, staring at Mudd. "Do you have a picture of the cherry tree?" he asked.

She shrugged a shoulder. "I'll ask Aunt B when I talk to her."

His focus switched to the green leafed, gray moss-dripping trees along the drive. They were older, like him. They didn't appear to be changed, unlike him. What was Miss B like now, and what did she think of him?

The change in him had been instant once he drove into Savannah. He was no longer the New Yorker he'd tried to become. He was a born and bred Southern boy, the caretaker's son. And sitting in that rocking chair was a relative of the owner of this antebellum mansion, offering him a job.

He felt a smile, and to make Miss Annabelle think it was about his dog, he reached over and played with the clay-red hair on Mudd's head.

Chapter 3

Annabelle wanted to ask how Symon felt about his dad dying. Likely, the way she felt about her own dad dying, so there was no need to ask. Had Miss B sent him a sympathy card? Did he have any other family? Where was his mother? She'd never seen a woman at the caretaker's cottage. Had never given it much thought. The caretaker and his son had been part of the property.

The last time she'd seen him up close was when she was just into her teen years and she sat in the backseat of Aunt B's town car with her mother while Symon, looking very much like a grown boy, drove them from the airport and talked with her dad, who sat in the front passenger seat.

That memory brought with it a recollection of resentment. She'd begun to notice boys, but this one didn't even glance at her through the rearview mirror. She quickly removed herself from that memory. It had been ridiculous then, a silly feeling of a thirteen-year-old. And it really didn't matter, anyway. Reminded her of the silly way SweetiePie and Mudd were acting around each other. Neither had a reason to be concerned about the other. Except…weren't cats and dogs supposed to be natural enemies?

But none of that had anything to do with her and Symon, the caretaker's son. He was a worker, she the employer. Well, not exactly though. It was more like he was doing her a favor. Was he a friend of Aunt B? Would she consider him a guest? Aunt B never mentioned him to her in a personal way. They'd had no reason to discuss him except on two occasions. One was when the caretaker had bouts with illness and Aunt B said the son had moved away. Then, after the caretaker died, Aunt B said Symon might come back again someday.

Annabelle didn't know why he would.

But now he was here.

She remembered him and his dad as the property's permanent fixtures, yet they'd been behind the scenes like Willamina.

No, not as visible as Willamina. She was like a servant at dinners or special occasions. But when Annabelle went into the kitchen and no other adults were around, Willamina became like a mama except she was sassy and her dark eyes threatened you not to cross her.

The caretaker and his son had never been sassy. She never heard them say a word except to give information about when repairmen would come, what window had cracked and needed to be replaced, when to be present upon the delivery of a new TV, computer or appliance.

"What all do you do?" she asked.

Annabelle detected an aloofness about him. The few times she'd been near him in the past she'd thought it was a subservient attitude. Now, she thought it was indifference—to her.

"Let's see." He looked up at the porch ceiling as if the answer lay there. Then he pointed to a stain she'd never noticed. "I could find out what caused that discoloration. Whether there's a place on the roof that caused a leak and can be fixed easily or if the entire porch needs new roofing. Or the entire house."

Annabelle groaned and shook her head. "Let's try things that take less time and expense."

He acknowledged that with a nod. "There's general maintenance that shows, like high grass and the weed beds."

She laughed when he looked at the flower bed in front of the banister. She remembered the beds used to look beautiful. She'd accepted them without thinking about how they got that way. Then last spring Aunt B brought in a landscaping service to get the beds ready. The same one her neighbors had used in Jones Square.

"I'm not sure what's weeds and what's flowers coming up."

His wry grin indicated it might be both.

"How long are you staying?" she asked.

"That depends on Miss B."

"Oh." He hadn't asked for a job. But...was that why he came here? To ask Aunt B for his daddy's job? Probably needed one to pay for that car. But that wasn't her business.

"I'll need the key to the storage room under the cottage."

"Do you know where it is?"

"If no one has stayed in the cottage, then I suppose it would be here in the house, in the laundry room on the keyboard."

She nodded. "There are some keys there. Just let me know."

"You want to give me your phone number?"

At her quick look, he spoke in a bland tone. "A phone call or text message might make things easier. That way I can let you know if I go to get fuel for the mower, if it needs to be repaired, if I should get mulch for the entire place or the front bed only, replace those banister slats that are warped and paint them or paint the entire banister. Little things like that."

She felt foolish. But then, what did she know about being an employer?

"If you prefer," he said, "I can come knocking on the door

when I have a question. Or we can use social media. Email. Facebook. Twitter—"

She laughed. "I get the picture. Why don't you just do the basics for now and after you see Aunt B we'll take it from there."

"Good enough." He grinned. "I'll start with the grass."

"I'll look for the key." She got up and went inside, shooed SweetiePie away, surprised at the way the cat was acting. Of course she knew SweetiePie was independent, but not an aggressor.

She got a key from the laundry room on the board beneath the initials SR and returned to the front porch.

He stood when she held it out.

"I assume SR stands for storage room," she said.

"Either that or Savannah River."

"Well, if it doesn't open the storage room, try the river."

He held out his hand and she dropped the key into his palm just as her phone rang. "Oh, I need to get that." Probably Wesley or Miss B.

Symon turned to go.

She opened the screen door and out streaked Sweetie Pie like white lightning. Mudd yelped and scuttled over the lawn, across the driveway, and tried to hide on the other side of the picket fence separating the big house lawn from the cottage yard.

"SweetiePie," Annabelle yelled, which did no good.

The cat looked at the dog cowering on the other side of the fence, then turned and sauntered back to where Annabelle was holding open the screen door and marched into the house as innocently as if nothing had happen.

"She's never done that before," Annabelle said.

"Has a dog been around before?"

"No."

"Maybe that's why she hasn't done it."

"Maybe." But she was doubtful. "She's a sweet cat. And

she was declawed when she was just a kitten. She's a house cat. Only goes to the porch or out to potty, when she doesn't use the litter box."

"Well," he said, "at least they have that much in common. The potty part, that is. But she does have fangs, you know. Mudd got more exercise today than he's used to, being holed up in an apartment."

Oh, so he had an apartment.

"And, she didn't hurt him. I suppose any self-respecting dog needs to be made aware of his boundaries. But I'll check to see if any damage was done to his legs. Hate for him to end up as a three-legged dog."

Was he serious? The dog had run with difficulty and his breathing sounded like fear or pain. SweetiePie might have sensed that since she didn't attack him or outrun him, which she could have. Before she could ask, the phone started ringing again.

She lifted a hand and hurried inside. By the time she got to the phone, it had stopped ringing. She ascended the stairs while listening to her messages. The first was from Megan, who said she needed to talk to her but it wasn't really urgent, just urgent.

The second was from Wesley, saying he had to be in a meeting, then a dinner, and would call her later tonight.

Seeing the time, she groaned. She'd have to rush to be at the mall by four. She looked out the window and SweetiePie jumped up onto the sill.

She watched Symon stroll to the storage room door, accompanied by the limping Mudd, who seemed none the worse for his trek across the lawn. They disappeared inside the room. The cat meowed and her blue eyes questioned.

Annabelle sunk her fingers into the soft fur on SweetiePie's head.

"Don't worry," she soothed. "They're only temporary."

Chapter 4

Inane, how a little girl not yet in school who had stuck her tongue out at him in Miss B's kitchen could evoke retaliatory emotions in a grown man.

Any resentment or jealousy had been childish. Now he'd have to describe his feelings as having been correct, based not on childishness but on a deep-seated sense of unfairness.

That sassy little girl had had free reign of Miss's B's house and grounds while he'd been relegated to the front steps or Willamina's kitchen. And unless he was helping his dad, he belonged on the other side of the picket fence.

Willamina's chillun, as she called them, came with her sometimes and could play with him down along the creek, but Annabelle wasn't allowed to go there. And he'd wondered if it was because of her age, the creek…or because of him. Did they think if she started to drown in the swollen creek he wouldn't save her?

He laughed and looked at Mudd for acknowledgment that he wasn't crazy for reverting to such a childhood memory. He likely would have been crazy had Miss B not recognized his overactive wild-story imagination and steered him toward the blank sheet of paper for working out the truth and meaning.

What had Annabelle's background made of her? What had that fancy little girl become? He could imagine most anything, but had difficulty seeing her scooping out a litter box. Maybe Willamina still worked there and did that chore.

The last time he'd seen Annabelle up close when he'd lived here she was just getting into her teen years. He drove her and her parents to Miss B's from the airport. He didn't look at her in case she stuck out her tongue. After all, he was eighteen then and ready for college. She was a kid.

She wasn't a kid any longer.

Now that he thought about it, he'd been aware of her picture in the paper when she won some kind of beauty pageant. He hadn't thought much about it, just turned the page to the sports section that had news about his swimming team.

But, if he'd met a girl like Annabelle in New York his approach would be quite different from sitting on the porch asking for a key so he could do her yard work. In New York, a girl would be asking to do his. Except he didn't have a yard to take care of in New York. He had a studio apartment in a concrete jungle and he preferred the caretaker's cottage any day.

But he didn't need to tell anybody that. He didn't need to tell anybody anything, come to think of it. He did tell Mudd a few secrets however and often ran a few thoughts by him.

"You'll be fine, boy," he said to Mudd, who stuck close to him, heeled in fact without being told. He'd been trained well. Probably missed his former owners. "We'll just need to steer clear of that feline. Seems she's relegated you to this side of the picket fence. I think she's more tease than threat. Time will tell."

He unlocked the storage room that filled most of the space beneath the cottage. The stale warm air was quite a contrast to the memory of mingled smells of wood, paint and tools. Even metal had its own odor.

Everything now lay mute and lifeless without his dad. The windows were dirty, something that never would have been had his daddy been alive. His daddy kept the tools and work tables as neat and clean as he did the property.

He could almost smell the earthy odor of his dad and hear him say, "Anything worth doing is worth doing right." And his dad had made him redo things more than once.

The riding mower was parked to the side on cardboard and the battery sat on a back shelf. Just from the looks of it, he knew his dad had been the last one to use it in the fall and had stored it for the winter. He checked anyway to confirm that the gas tank and the oil had been drained.

He made a mental list of supplies he'd need. "Come on, Mudd," he said. "Let's take a look at the creek. There's much more room here than the few feet of dirt behind the shrubs at the apartment in New York."

Glancing back at the big house he saw the white ball of fur stretched out on a second-floor window sill, looking comfortable and self-satisfied, and her face turned toward them. Mudd looked, too, and whimpered.

"You're fine. Just stay on this side of the fence."

He could almost hear his dad telling him about the landscaping, what they needed to do to keep the creek from flooding the yard after a hard rain. At certain places they'd placed boulders and a selection of plants that combined with the natural growth, providing a lush oasis while another section was a peaceful place to sit on the bench and read or make up stories while propped up on boulders or against a tree. The path along the creek needed to be tended, to keep the natural look without being overgrown. Tree roots needed to be checked for damage.

Symon realized how much his dad had taught him just by talking as they worked. He'd considered it all research for what he put into his stories. Standing there now, beneath moss-laden trees and smelling the creek, he experienced pleasure, a desire to work in the dirt with his hands. He wanted to clean out the unnecessary underbrush, clear out the vines that tended to take over. Remove spindly and diseased trees. It looked as if no work had been done here in over two years.

His dad had introduced him to fishing for panfish in that creek. Also how to clean and cook it. And the eating was nothing to sneeze at. He hadn't fished in years. Mudd might enjoy it, too. Maybe a dip in the deeper part of the creek. Symon used to swim in it, pretending he was a salmon going upstream.

Strange, the place he wanted to get away from now beckoned like bait to a panfish.

He was a free spirit. Yes, like moss that floated in the air. And then the oak trees beckoned and the moss made them its home.

Home.

His dad had taught him he could be a landscaper, a caretaker of top quality. But Symon had wanted to be like Miss B, a person in a big house who paid the caretaker.

Now, as Symon and Mudd walked around to the front door of the cottage, he glanced back at the big house and smiled. No, now that he could own a big house with its long drive and spacious lawns if he wanted to, he rather preferred something like this cozy cottage tucked away amid lush green cypress, sourwood that would soon exhibit drooping white spike clusters and live oaks draped with Spanish moss. Summer annuals needed to be planted in Miss B's flower beds. They would be beautiful against the backdrop of boxwoods and azaleas.

The front door was unlocked, as if waiting for him. Miss B had written that he was always welcome to return here. An instant of dread passed over him as he walked into the cottage where he hadn't been in over two years. Then, he'd been filled with the emotions of having to dispose of his dad's ashes. No funeral, no remembrance; his dad would be forgotten after Symon packed anything of his own to take away. He'd left a note saying that Willamina or anyone else could do as they wished with his dad's few belongings, which were just clothes and shoes. Symon had scattered his dad's ashes and told himself that part of his life was over.

Now, however, standing in the living room, he felt the absence of the man who'd always been there. The man who'd kept his son. Had he wanted him, or had he just not known what to do with him after his wife left?

He opened the living room windows, bypassed his dad's office and bedroom, and went into the room that had been his. It felt warm, looked rather bare but clean. He opened the windows, wanting the cool spring breeze, the scent of the creek and the foliage. His dad always said he could smell the plants growing.

Mudd sniffed around, as if smelling something. Symon did not detect the odor of soap. His dad always washed up at the sink in the storage room before coming up to the living quarters and had taught Symon to do that, too. He remembered his dad touched him, rumpled his hair, clasped his shoulder, even bent to tuck in him in at night when he very young. But that had changed. The bottle had replaced Symon. Miss B tried explaining it to Symon years ago.

"The hardest thing in the world to do after you lose someone so close is to go on," she said. "A person has to work at looking to what he still has, instead of what he has lost. Sometimes it takes years, or even a lifetime, to let it go. And sometimes you can't let it go at all."

Symon hadn't understood that. However, now he knew he'd lived it.

He felt a little of it now. His dad seemed closer now that he was gone than when they'd been together all the time.

His dad had said one time, "Put your stories down if you want to, boy, but you're going to learn how to make a living. I'm teaching you to work with your hands, how to fix things. You think this isn't much. Well, it's a living. And a pretty good one."

"The house is not ours," Symon had said.

His dad had scoffed, "Most people's houses belong to the bank, they just call it theirs because they signed a paper to pay the bank. You already know more than a lot of landscapers. You can get a job as a landscaper, or a caretaker, or even start your own business. You've had years of experience. And you can't depend on those stories to bring in a dime."

Practical, that's what he was.

And now, Symon realized he was right.

He'd helped his dad when needed, mainly at the beginning of spring and in the fall while in high school. In the summer, Symon worked as a swimming coach for children and a lifeguard on Tybee Island. But while in college he didn't work at landscaping jobs.

He'd thought of the work on Miss B's property as just that—work.

Now, the thought of it brought a sense of pleasure, like getting back to his roots.

Even though Miss B had written "the cottage is still your home" two years ago when she sent a sympathy card, it really wasn't.

It was Miss B's cottage.

Four years ago, he'd brought his dad and Miss B his first book, widely acclaimed at the time.

His dad had said it had a nice cover and asked if he was making any money off it.

"Not yet," Symon had said.

Miss B had grasped it as if it was precious and said she wasn't at all surprised his first book was published and doing well. She shouldn't have been. She was the one who had taught him.

After that, he sent her his books when they came out. She'd

always sent a note of thanks. Polite. Saying the cottage was there. He was always welcome. She was proud of him. She'd never written that she appreciated his dedicating his books to her. Maybe she didn't appreciate books about killers.

Even if she didn't, surely she would welcome his taking care of some of the dire needs of the property. It was definitely in need of more than surface work. He'd get the supplies needed for the riding mower and the work on the grounds, stock the refrigerator, put a few things in the cabinets, and ask at the fitness center about opening and closing times and the pool schedule for adult laps.

Having plans under way, he took in his laptop and set it on the desk in his dad's office.

Already his mind was working overtime with story possibilities. He wouldn't mind doing a little research on Miss Annabelle. What was an attractive young woman her age doing living with Miss B? Why was there no engagement or wedding ring on her finger? What lay behind that pretty face? That was fodder for some kind of story.

But for now, for some strange reason, he felt more like a landscaper looking forward to breathing the aroma of freshly mowed grass and getting his hands in the dirt than he did typing on a blank screen.

He'd begin his new project after he got the picture, not that he needed it, of the cherry tree.

And as much as he knew he'd enjoy it, landscaping was temporary. But he'd begun to long for more than temporary things, especially relationships. He needed to know if Miss B could feel about him now like she did when he was a boy and a young man. She'd said he was her pleasure, her joy. And he'd looked upon her as a perfect kind of mom.

Chapter 5

Annabelle called and told Aunt B she'd drive out and visit with her and Clovis for a little while. It was only a twenty-minute drive, but Tybee was like a world away from the trees, spacious lawns and rocking chairs on Aunt B's front porch. Annabelle liked evening walks along the beach.

When she drove up, she saw the two women sitting at a table on the balcony. Annabelle drove underneath it and parked. She walked up the steps and through the house then opened the glass doors.

"Hey," Clovis said as soon as Annabelle opened the glass doors and her heels clicked across the wooden deck to enjoy Clovis's hug and Aunt B's welcome.

"Oh, you're so cute," Clovis said.

Annabelle glanced down at her silk blouse and conservative skirt just above her knees, typical of what she wore to her job at the modeling studio. "Smell good, too," Clovis said. "Like fresh shampoo. But you're still skinny. I have just the thing."

She lifted a finger and went inside.

Annabelle felt her large gold loop earrings brush against her face as she bent her head and reached into her tote for a book. "Here's the third one. Came in today."

"Oh, another in the series by DiAnn Mills." She stroked the cover. "One of my favorites," she said.

Annabelle smiled, knowing her aunt didn't claim to have a favorite author but tried to teach her students to appreciate a beginning writer with story as well as a seasoned writer with technique, and those who exhibited both. "Clovis and I like to read in the heat of the day and at night."

Annabelle pulled out a chair and sat. "I have good news. Somebody's going to do your yard work." She spoke with confidence. "And it's not going to cost a cent."

Aunt B's eyebrows rose. "No cost?"

Annabelle held up a hand. "I know, Aunt B. Nothing is free. The worker does get to stay in the caretaker's cottage."

Her aunt's breath was audible.

"Is that all right? He just wants to stay in the cottage for…I think he said a short while." Now she wondered if she'd done the wrong thing.

"Well." Aunt B didn't seem pleased. "As long as he takes care of it."

Annabelle nodded. "I told him that." She grimaced. "He does have a dog," she said and quickly added, "But it seems well-mannered."

"What about SweetiePie?"

She fluffed that off with a toss of her hand. "The dog's name is Mudd and it gets around about as fast as one plowing through a mud puddle. No problem about SweetiePie."

They shared a laugh. Then Aunt B turned thoughtful. "How is he going to fare without wages?"

Annabelle shrugged. "I didn't ask. I mean, he seems self-sufficient. Drives a sports car. Said he'd like to rent the cottage. He's your former caretaker's son."

"What?" Aunt B raised her hand to her chest as if she had a thundering heart. She breathed, "He's back. He came back. Oh." Her breath was labored. "How is he? What's he like? How does he look?" She took a deep breath and exhaled slowly. Annabelle thought she was going to come out of her chair, or her skin. "I mean, I haven't seen him in years."

Was Aunt B glad, or not? She muttered, "Grown-up... nice I guess.... Why? I mean..." She leaned over the table. "Did I do wrong?"

Her aunt was grasping the book as if it would fly away. She loosened her grip and laid the book on the table. "I—I... Just tell me what he said."

Her aunt was never this discombobulated. "He said he came to see the cherry tree."

"Oh, my." Aunt B pressed her hand against her ribs. "Oh, don't make me laugh."

Annabelle was glad to hear the sliding of the glass door. She rose to help Clovis but kept a watchful eye on Aunt B. This was a side of her aunt she was not accustomed to.

As if nothing were amiss, the three of them settled at the table with tea and cookies. Annabelle filled Clovis in on the conversation about the caretaker. After a sip of tea, Annabelle's face turned thoughtful. "Come to think of it, he seemed upset about the tree being cut down."

Aunt B chuckled. "So he came to see the cherry tree."

Annabelle nodded, her eyes questioning. "He wanted to know if I had a picture of the tree." She spread her hands. "I said I'd ask you."

Aunt B took a long drink of the tea and set the glass down. "You could probably find many pictures of the tree in my albums."

"Is it all right to let him— Come to think of it, isn't that a strange request?"

Aunt B said, "Rather mild, considering..."

Annabelle speculated. "Maybe it has some kind of sentimental value. I mean, maybe his dad planted it or something." She shrugged.

Aunt B smiled and looked at her tea but didn't respond to that. Then she looked across again. "Did he say anything else?"

"He did ask about you. But didn't talk about himself. I didn't think I should pry."

Aunt B smiled. "Tell him I'm delighted he's here and he's welcome to stay in the cottage as long as he likes. And he doesn't have to do the yard work to stay there." She looked happy about the whole thing. "If he wants to see me right away he's welcome to come out here. But I'll be back in a few days."

Annabelle nodded. "What if he doesn't plan to stay that long?"

"He will. Otherwise he wouldn't have come and asked to rent the cottage."

Clovis smiled faintly, then looked at her tea. Annabelle was trying to absorb the situation when Aunt B changed the subject. "No dinner with Wesley tonight?"

Annabelle sighed heavily. "He's working late again on that big murder trial. They're not even breaking for dinner tonight. Having something brought in. But—" Her hands lifted as if in praise. "I'll see him Friday night. Then over the weekend." She sneered playfully. "Looks like I don't need an excuse not to work on that book project for Celeste."

"Oh, and another thing, Annabelle, about Symon," Aunt B said, returning to that subject again. "Don't make him feel like a worker. He's my…guest."

Chapter 6

The sound jerked her upright in bed as if someone had tied a string around her and pulled her to a sitting position. Sweetie-Pie yowled and jumped out from under the covers. The saliva caught in Annabelle's throat and gave her a coughing fit. That was not the bird calls, chirping and singing she usually awakened to at dawn. A whirring roar stabbed her consciousness like a helicopter landing on the grounds.

She had no morning prayer of thanks for the birds or cool morning air stirring the lace curtains. Tossing back the comforter and sheet, she swung her legs around to the side of the bed and stepped onto the carpeted floor. Wide awake from the sudden shock, she scooped up SweetiePie, went to the window and peered out at the riding lawn mower rolling along the edge of the brick patio.

Awake then, she realized the sound wasn't so loud after all, just different and unexpected to her sleep-induced state of mind.

Atop the mower sat that raven-haired man in a T-shirt

and jeans, now headed for the edge of the lawn. Steering the mower didn't take a lot of effort, but she was aware of his wide shoulders and muscular physique. But she'd known that yesterday. He'd started working early, she'd give him that. He made his turn and began the second row across the yard.

When he reached the spot below her window, one hand lifted in a wave. But he didn't look up. Maybe he'd glimpsed her as he'd proceeded her way. She stepped back as if he was looking at her in the cami and short pajamas. She chuckled at that. She was as covered now as she had been when they'd talked yesterday, especially since she was now holding long-white-furred SweetiePie close.

Miss Independence jumped to the floor. She'd be ready for her breakfast since she couldn't jump to the windowsill and fantasize about the birds in the trees.

While dressing for the morning, Annabelle reprimanded herself for thinking he didn't look like a caretaker's son. What did she think he should look like? Ugly? Scrawny? She needed to work on her perceptions. In fact, she was beginning to remember having glimpsed him in her younger years. Seems he'd been on a high school swimming team—before she started high school, so it hadn't mattered. Not that it would have, anyway.

She remembered seeing him sitting by the creek when she'd wandered down that far. She'd watched for a while, wondering why he sat so still and what he had to think about.

During breakfast of cereal with banana slices, she thought about Aunt B's future, and her own for that matter. Each of them had changes taking place. Aunt B was retiring from teaching and Annabelle was considering going into teaching. Aunt B's lifestyle would change now that she had retired. Annabelle had options to consider about her own future. And a lot depended on when Wesley might make junior partner.

Right now, however, she needed to find a picture. After rinsing out her bowl and putting it into the dishwasher, she got the photo albums from the bookshelf in Aunt B's bed-room and took them to the kitchen table. Over a second cup of coffee, she looked through them.

There was one of a cute little boy with dark unruly hair stretching out his arm to hold on to the trunk of the small tree and looking like he owned the world with that little chin raised and eyes staring. Maybe five or six years old? Was that Symon? She remembered him as a young boy, but not that young.

There were a few of the tree at different sizes in the back-ground of photos of family members and Aunt B's friends. In one, the tree was bare. Why had Aunt B, or someone, taken a picture of the bare tree? "Oh." She stopped turning pages. There was one of the full-grown tree, with its deep pink blos-soms. Perhaps Aunt B had taken them because of the contrast.

Annabelle slipped the blossoming tree from its plas-tic pocket, put it in a freezer bag and laid it on the table. She could hear the mower in the front yard. That eventu-ally stopped.

A short while later, she opened the wooden door and saw Symon pulling up weeds in the grossly neglected flower bed in front of the banister.

Making sure SweetiePie wasn't with her, she opened the screen and walked out onto the porch. "SweetiePie's inside," she said.

Mudd was already on his way toward the cottage.

Symon said, "Come," and the dog stopped, obviously un-certain whether to come or go.

"He's not sure he can trust you," she said.

"It's the cat he doesn't trust. Or…you."

"Me? I wouldn't a hurt a flea."

"Maybe that's his reasoning. He'd prefer you hurt those fleas."

She scrunched her nose. "He has fleas?"

"No New York fleas. I'll need to find a vet to see if he has any Savannah ones."

She started to laugh but thought he was probably serious. "I can recommend SweetiePie's vet."

He glanced up. She wasn't sure if that look meant he wasn't about to take Mudd to SweetiePie's vet, or if he already knew about vets. "Unless you know where to take him."

"I'm sure the feline's vet will do." He kept working.

"You don't have to work yourself to death, you know."

His hand lifted. "Not at all. There's something soothing about the smell of freshly mown grass, and dirt, don't you think?"

She considered that. "I haven't had much experience with dirt. But compared to exhaust fumes, not to mention river smells, tour buses, guests who are warm from what they call our humid weather, yes, I reckon there is. There's something peaceful about being out here at Aunt B's."

"You don't live here?"

"I live in the center of a square, you might say. With a couple friends. I'm using the excuse of house-sitting while Aunt B is away. I could just come and go. I do that often anyway since she had a room in the basement transformed into an exercise room."

"The one that used to have mirror and bar where you practiced your ballet?"

"You know about that?"

"Caretaking isn't just landscaping. Part of my dad's job was to arrange for repairs to be done, install things and be around in case of any infringement on security measures. My dad insisted I learn every aspect of the business."

"I see," she said, although she hadn't thought of their work as being a business. But of course it was. She and her friends had a list of who to call for what. And there was always something.

Should she say he was welcome to use the exercise room?

No, better not. After all, she was staying there alone. "I have a few things to think about and this is a good place for it."

"I agree," he said. "That's one reason I've come back."

He glanced up, reached over for a bottle of water, downed it, then stood. His hand moved to the neck of his sweat-soaked T-shirt and he made a fanning motion. "I'd forgotten how humid it gets here." A golden gleam appeared in his dark eyes and she knew it wasn't because of her. She was in as bad shape as he, wearing what she wore yesterday and probably smelling of sweat, too. He glanced at the photo. "Is that what I think it is?"

"The cherry tree."

He bent down for a cloth lying on the ground and wiped his hands, then straightened and reached for the bag. She leaned over the banister and he took it.

"What do you want it for?"

He stared at the picture. "I want to look at it. And think."

Well, at least he wasn't thinking about her. Not that she wanted him to. But she'd never have suspected a guy might prefer looking at a picture of a cherry tree to looking at her. Wesley wouldn't.

"You want me to put the picture up here on the table?"

"Yes, please." He handed it to her. "Obviously, you told Miss B I'm here."

"Let's see," she mused, looking out at the velvety lawn, then back again at his level gaze. "She was pleased. Said you are welcome to stay. And you're not obligated to work."

"In that case—" He brushed at the dirt on the knees of his pants. "You can finish up here."

Gaping at him, she stepped back from the banister.

"However," he said and picked up the empty water bottle. "You refill this for me and I'll consider getting this bed ready for a colorful array of spring like you've never seen."

She closed her open mouth and took the bottle, then turned

and put the picture on the table. Going inside and filling the bottle, she began to wonder if she needed to lighten up a bit and not take every word from a person's mouth seriously.

She returned and handed him the water, which he began to drink. "By the way, Aunt B said she'll be back in a few days but if you want to visit with her at Tybee, that's fine."

He nodded.

"Oh," she said, just then thinking of it. "I could give you wages if you want. I mean, you do have to eat."

A stiff look settled on his face. "Miss B said that?"

An immediate thought was that he was as sensitive as Mudd. And Aunt B made it plain he was not a worker but a guest. Well, if he could say silly things while acting serious, so could she.

She looked around and made her eyes question. "I'm pretty sure Aunt B isn't here, and that sounded a lot like me, so it must have been me, I mean, it must have been I who said it."

She felt reasonably sure that was a grin forming at the corner of his full wide lips. Then he suddenly looked serious again and his brow, with that wayward wisp of hair falling over it, furrowed.

"That's kind of you, Miss Annabelle. But would you believe I found a pirate's treasure in the backyard? Mudd sniffed it out like a trained dog would sniff out a cadaver, so he dug down, wondering what might be buried down there and lo and behold there was a pirate's chest, full of treasure. Should keep me in food for a while. But thanks for thinking of me." He lifted a hand with his index finger pointing. "Finders keepers, you know."

Annabelle laughed. Strange fellow, him. That expression she'd noticed before appeared in his slate-colored eyes. She couldn't tell if it was a condescending look or an evaluating one. A measuring kind of look, as if he was trying to see into her soul, or at least asking, *What are you? Who are you?*

Her answer would have to be, *I don't really know.*

Lest he try and make her walk some kind of imaginary plank, she decided to play along. "Please keep whatever treasure you find, as long as it doesn't mean digging up the lawn you've just made look so pretty and smell so good."

He nodded. "Thanks."

"You're welcome." She turned quickly, knowing her tone didn't sound welcome.

She went inside and closed the screen door, then peered over her shoulder at him. He'd already kneeled down, concentrating on the flower bed. For some strange reason he made her feel like he was laughing at her. That was silly. Why would she care anyway what a...a caretaker's son thought of her?

No matter how good-looking he happened to be!

Chapter 7

Not again!

After she'd anticipated this all day. All week, really.

Annabelle sat in one of the rockers on the front porch with her eyes closed, trying to assuage that feeling of disquiet since Wesley's call. Hearing a car door shut she looked to her right and saw Symon turn his head her way. He lifted a hand, then switched on the engine, drove down the drive several feet, stopped and backed up.

SweetiePie, who'd been rolling around beneath the banister, sat up and looked. Mudd stared from the backseat and when SweetiePie rose up, he ducked down out of sight. Coward, that animal.

Symon turned off the engine and got out, then approached her. He looked good in his jeans and knit top. He stood at the bottom of the steps, next to the flower beds now devoid of weeds and ready for whatever he might do to them next. "Hi," he said.

She echoed, "Hi."

"Thought I'd go out for a bite to eat. You recommend any place?"

Remembering his quip about treasure, she shrugged and widened her eyes, trying to look as if it would be obvious. "The Pirate's Cave. On River Street."

He scoffed, "I'm not giving up my treasure chest."

Annabelle laughed. "Believe me, they have plenty."

He nodded. "If you're not otherwise occupied, want to show me where that is?"

She knew he probably knew, having lived here. "Do I look otherwise occupied?"

"Well, yes. Like you're enjoying all this peace and quiet." That little twitch occurred at his mouth, as if one of these days he might really grin.

"Frankly," she said, "I'm fuming. Friday night is my big night out, but my fiancé just called and said he's working late."

"Umh" accompanied his single nod, could well be saying she didn't exactly look ready for a big night out, dressed in beige knee-length shorts and a raspberry-colored short-sleeved knit sweater. She and Wes had their share of dressing up and going out. And Wes had worked particularly hard and long hours in the past few weeks. They both had looked forward to this night being in Aunt B's house, alone, talking about their future, maybe watching a movie and just enjoying each other.

Symon followed that "Umh" with, "That happens."

"No." She laughed lightly, beginning to catch on to his different way of communicating. "It's not an excuse. It's real."

He lifted a finger. "Ah, that's not what I was thinking. I was thinking that you've established you have a fiancé. Even if you forgot to put on your ring."

She gasped. "You're terrible. Don't you know a commitment is more than something one wears on a finger?"

"Sure," he said. "It's something like we have for Miss B.

We've both known her for a long time, you know. We're not exactly strangers here." He looked off to his left and sang softly, quite well, "Should auld acquaintance be forgot, and never brought to mind."

She laughed. "We weren't exactly friends."

He looked at her beneath narrowed lids. "Acquaintances," he said. "Worlds apart."

She thought of that. She'd felt privileged, thought he was poor. She hadn't given it conscious thought, but his dad had been Aunt B's employee. A fact. But he'd lived on this property. She'd visited. And what was he doing here…now? Her mind questioned, *Who is he and what is he?*

That quickly changed to, *Who am I? What am I?*

Avoiding any kind of answer, she rose from the rocker. "I'll put SweetiePie inside, and be right with you."

He turned. "I'll put Mudd in the cottage."

Establishing SweetiePie inside and making sure she had food in her dish, Annabelle wondered what Symon was to Miss B. She'd seemed elated that he had returned, as if it was some wonderful event. And she'd said not to treat him like a worker, but a guest. She would do this…for Aunt B.

When she went to the car, he remained in the driver's seat but leaned over and opened the passenger door for her. With one glance inside she was aware of the awesome contrast of the slate gray interior with the tawny color seats. She sank into the comfortable leather and fastened her seat belt.

She looked over at him. "This," she said, "is gorgeous."

"Thank you," he said. "My only luxury. Other than Mudd, of course."

She rather expected to smell dog. Instead, she smelled leather. The car might be fairly new. And mingled with it was a hint of what? Not cologne or aftershave. Maybe soap or shampoo? She smiled, thinking he didn't seem the kind to wear a fragrance, or at least not a very noticeable one.

His black leopard purred down the long drive and out to

the road. "Could we stop by Jones Street? I want to pick up a few things."

"You mean rob the place?" He widened his eyes in mock excitement. "Sounds like this will be anything but dull."

She laughed. This was much better than sitting around sulking about not seeing Wesley until later, if then. "Well, we could break in, but since I have a key I might as well use it."

The way his attention quickly turned to talking about the squares, the architecture of the historic homes made her realize how much she took for granted. Many times she'd driven along the streets, taking for granted all her blessings. His words punctuated that thought. "There are some really nice homes on Jones Street."

"I've roomed there with two of my friends since college days. Except for a few weeks after my parents were killed."

His head turned to her. "I didn't know that. How long ago?"

"About three years. Oh, turn left, then go straight. Aunt B was my lifesaver."

"I know the feeling," he returned.

There it was again, the implication of a relationship with Aunt B that Annabelle didn't know about.

In between telling him where to turn, she told him briefly about the accident. The speeding truck driver had failed to stop at the stop sign and ran into the driver's side of the car. The car rolled over. Her dad, her mom and the driver were killed. The truck driver's cell phone indicated he'd been in the middle of a text message.

"I'm sorry," he said.

She nodded but didn't speak as he turned onto the brick street. For a moment she felt rather like one of those bricks was on her chest. But the feeling would pass. Aunt B had forced her to focus on the good memories. "Okay, a couple houses down." She pointed to the left. "The one with the twin set of steps and the flag over the railing of the entry. The palmetto bush in front."

"Got it," he said, and slowed.

"Turn in and park at the back. Then we can walk to River Street and not have to find a parking place there, which is impossible anyway."

He did and she went up the steps and in the back way. She went into her bedroom and gathered the clothes she'd wear to the studio in the morning and few other items. Returning to the back of the house, seeing Symon walking around, studying the view, waiting for her, she felt a little guilty for feeling good about this when Wes was working. He didn't like long hours any more than she.

But she did have to eat. And there'd probably be more wrong with staying on the front porch than being friendly with Aunt B's…whatever he was. Not worker. Friend? Guest?

"I wiped away all the fleas," Symon said. He took the items and laid them across the narrow backseat. He locked the car with the remote and they began to walk around the house.

It occurred to her that the caretaker's cottage could compare with the houses on Jones Street, in beauty and history. Maybe it was even more favorable in location. But not in size and grandeur compared with Aunt B's antebellum home.

"Is this where your family lived?" he asked.

"Couple houses away," she said. "And they had a place on Tybee." She sighed, thinking of having gone through the financial situation with attorneys about her dad's part of the law firm, and eventually selling everything that hadn't been paid for, and leaving her with a small inheritance. "This house belongs to Megan's grandmother. She's in a nursing home now. Megan, Lizzie and I rent it. We get along great."

She laughed. "Maybe one reason is we rarely see each other. Megan has a steady guy named Michael. She leads afternoon and evening historic tours. Lizzie wants desperately to find Mr. Right, but hasn't yet. You'll meet her at the Pirate's Cave. Her family owns it."

He nodded. "What does your fiancé do?" he said as they walked around the side of the house. "If you don't mind my asking."

"No reason to mind." She looked up at him. He was tall. Taller than Wes. Maybe a half foot taller than she. "Wesley is an attorney with the Yarwood Law Firm."

"Ah," Symon said. "Your dad's firm."

Yes, he would know that. "Wes has been there less than a year and is hoping to become junior partner. His loyalty for the firm seems to be tested constantly, if you know what I mean."

He acknowledged that with another nod. "Working his way up, huh?"

"He's trying. Wesley hopes to be a senior partner someday. Maybe even go into politics."

"Like Miss B's dad," he said.

An attorney like her dad. A state senator like her granddad. "Yes," she said slowly. Those weren't his reasons, but if so, they were good ones. "Once he proves his worth, he won't have such an erratic schedule."

"Time and effort," he says. "That's what it takes."

Suddenly he stopped and looked up. Her gaze followed his. "What?" she said.

"Just absorbing all this. I had to get away to really appreciate it. Not take it for granted. It's all I knew when I was young."

"I suppose I sort of take it for granted, too. You're right. It is beautiful. I haven't walked along the squares in a long time. I think of it as being for the tourists. I suppose we can thank Sherman for not destroying it during the Civil War."

"And those who keep it beautiful."

"Like…landscapers?" she asked coyly.

He grinned at her. "That, too. There's not a lot of demand

for landscapers where I live. Just concrete sweepers. But they keep the cement looking wonderfully gray."

Surely he wasn't a street sweeper. "Where do you live?"

"New York."

"What do you do there? I mean, your occupation."

"I write."

"What do you write?"

"Novels. Mysteries. Thrillers."

"Oh. Like *Midnight in the Garden of Good and Evil* that was filmed here in Savannah?" She laughed.

He didn't. "Not exactly. Nothing made into a movie yet."

Ooops. She should be more careful. Everyone knew being in the arts was a hard way to make a living.

"Sorry..." she said low.

He chuckled then. "No problem." That look came onto his face again. Just a hint of amusement or reserve or something that gave her that uneasy feeling. He was...different. From what, she didn't know. Well, yes, she did. From those who tried to impress her. How many times she'd grown tired of others trying to impress her. Now that this one didn't, she wondered about it.

She'd walked this street, these squares, these cobbled stones, and she'd seen the statues, but somehow as Symon began to talk about them, it was as if she'd never really thought about them before. Sort of as if she'd taken her parents for granted until they were gone.

Symon pointed out, and she noticed how the lazy afternoon sun cast slanting shadows and made lacy patterns as they strolled along. The azaleas were abundant with buds ready to burst forth with their vivid hues of purple, pink and white. New life, ready to happen.

Then he said, "Do you know how Savannah got its name?"

She thought. Surely she'd read that. Studied that. But somehow the knowledge eluded her. "From the Savannah River?"

His look was playful and seemed to say, "Try again," so

she said, "Oh, the Savannah River would get its name from the city. Okay, a general? No..." He waited as she pursed her lips in thought, then gave him a sidelong look. "Savannah's a Native American name, isn't it?"

"Where did you go to school?" He shook his head. "A private one?"

"Frankly, yes."

He shrugged. "So did I. Miss B's private school."

She knew Aunt B had no private school, but she was rather enjoying his playful manner. "Tell me," she said. She liked his voice. Deep, resonant, precise, as if he were an accomplished speaker, and yet warm, informative. She could tell he liked to talk. She liked to listen.

"I was about five years old," he began and as he talked she could see it, feel it, and she pictured that little boy she'd seen in Aunt B's picture album.

"I had just told Miss B a lie so she began to educate me. She asked if I knew what a myth was. I thought it might be something like a hickory stick I'd seen Willamina use to switch her children. But I just looked down, feeling dumb as the board on the front porch that was good for nothing but to be walked on."

Annabelle laughed lightly. "Sensitive, weren't you?"

"Very. She didn't use a hickory stick, but my daddy made it clear that one word from her and he could lose his job. Anyway, Miss B kept on talking, like it didn't matter if I didn't know things."

He stopped when Annabelle chuckled. "Go on," she prompted.

"Well, she told me a myth is a story. Sometimes there's truth in it, sometimes not. She said a little girl about my age didn't mind her parents and went down to the creek." Symon shook his head. "I didn't like stories about children not minding their parents. They always got punished."

She laughed again when he placed his hand on his backside as if remembering.

"Well, the creek was swollen by the hard rains like Miss B's creek gets sometimes. And this little girl decided to rock hop. The mother went down and saw her daughter in a deep part with her clothing caught on a tree limb. She started screaming, *Save Anna. Save Anna!*"

Annabelle waited. Finally she asked, "Is that the end?"

He squinted. "I don't know. My mind went off in another direction. I saw a dark shape in the shadows near that creek. The little girl wasn't there all by herself. After going back to the cottage, I drew a picture of it and later wrote a story about it."

Skeptical, Annabelle lifted her face to his. "Aunt B told you that?"

His eyes widened. "Absolutely. But like you, I was skeptical. Miss B asked me if I thought 'Save Anna' sounded like Savannah. I sat there thinking. So she said it real fast and asked me again and I said, 'Yessum,' and she looked at me real sharp so I changed that to 'Yes, ma'am.'"

Annabelle had to stop and hold her stomach while she laughed. He remained stone-faced and kept on. "Miss B started talking about myths and some things being true and some not and it was acceptable to make up stories if you're going to entertain someone but not acceptable if they are asking for the truth. She was trying to teach me the difference between the truth and a lie. I had just told her a whopper."

She kept pace with him as he started walking again. "Ah," he said, "it's good to be back and remember those days."

"Why did you leave?"

"I went to New York right out of college and got a job with a publishing company. Seemed the place to start if one wanted to be a writer. Now, I realize I can write anywhere. Mudd and I are thinking about getting out of New York."

Oh, so that must be his main reason for being here. "I've been told I should write a book," she said. "About my occupation."

"And what's that? What do you do?" he asked as they reached River Street, which was crowded as usual. He stepped behind her and gently touched her waist as they let a man, woman and young child pass them on the sidewalk.

A feathery touch. And it seemed the spring breeze turned a mite cool and made her shiver. Why wasn't Wesley here with her? Why couldn't he enjoy this, too? He should be here.

Chapter 8

Normally, Annabelle didn't even have to think about the answer when someone asked what she did. Most people knew, anyway. But she felt like her life would sound rather boring after hearing the way he described even the most minute thing.

Others stepped aside to let them pass. They came to the statue of the waving girl. "I guess you know her story," Annabelle said.

He smiled and nodded. "What Miss B didn't teach me, she had me read. Yes, I know the waving girl's story."

"Miss B taught you?"

"Not in her classroom," he said. "On her front porch."

Annabelle had not known that.

"Didn't you go to public school?"

"Oh, yes. But she taught things I'd never learn in school."

"Like…what?"

"Like the story of the girl, waving goodbye to her lover

who never returned. Perhaps hoping it was a welcome home."
He looked at her. "How did you learn about her?"

Annabelle thought for a moment; then she laughed. "Probably heard it first from Aunt B."

They walked on down to the Pirate's Cave. He opened the door, stepped aside for her to enter. Even before her eyes adjusted to the dimness inside, she heard "Arrgh?" as if it were a question. She knew the inflection in Lizzie's growl was indeed a question.

The next sound was Lizzie with her pirate accent. "Welcome tae ye, mateys. Right this way."

Lizzie led them to a booth and Annabelle slid in opposite Symon. She looked up at Lizzie, dressed as usual in a pirate's outfit and with a bandanna around her head of long auburn hair.

Symon played the game. "Well, shiver me timbers. And who might ye be?"

"Veronica," Lizzie said, sounding rather British. "The Red Lady. I'm from the sixteenth century. Most of the time I pretend to be an entertainer or singer. I board the ships and at the first opportunity I take off my disguise. Underneath I'm wearing a shirt, pants and weapons. I kill everyone aboard and then sail out to sea."

"Right up my alley," Symon said. "Perhaps you could use a second mate."

Lizzie looked delighted, and lost her facade and her accent for a moment. "Worth considering," she said.

Goodness gracious. Were they flirting with each other? Annabelle knew Lizzie was desperate for a…mate. But she didn't know about Symon. Annabelle spread her hand toward her. "My friend and housemate, Lizzie."

She knew Lizzie would be wondering what in the world Annabelle was doing there with a…a man. But he wasn't just a man. "This is—" now she was the hesitant one "—Symon

Sinclair." She couldn't very well add that he was the caretaker's son.

"Nice to meet you, Symon," Lizzie said with a sly green-eyed gaze at Annabelle.

"He's…"

What?

"A friend, I mean a guest. Um, he came to see Aunt B."

Her glance moved to Symon, who seemed to be wearing that amused expression again. She reached for the menu still in Lizzie's hands.

"It's a pleasure to meet a lady pirate, Miss Lizzie," he said. "Particularly one who growls."

Lizzie laughed with him but not without that questioning glance at Annabelle.

"And what she means," Symon said, "is that I'm doing some work on Miss B's property and staying in the caretaker's cottage. In fact, I'm the former caretaker's son."

"Ooh. Caretaker's son," Lizzie said in thoughtful response. "My brother used to talk about Aunt B's—she's not my aunt, but I call her that—caretaker's son. Did you play football for the Dogs?"

Annabelle looked from Lizzie to Symon. He shook his head. "I was on the swim team."

"Oh, yeah," Lizzie said. "My brother talked about you. He was on the team. A couple years below you. Went to nationals in California, I think. You were their best swimmer, weren't you?"

"For a short period in my life, yes. Does your brother still swim?"

"Nope. Well, not on a team or anything. Like me, he pirates. But Paul's not here tonight."

Annabelle looked from one to the other as they laughed.

"I give tours of this cave, in case you're interested," Lizzie offered.

"I'm interested," Symon said.

"It takes a while," Annabelle said, looking over at Symon. This must be her night for abandonment. She lifted a hand as if in dismissal. "But you can take the tour if you want. After we eat I can walk back to the house. There's always something I can do there." She smirked. "Like laundry."

"Walk back alone?" Symon lifted his eyebrows.

"It's broad daylight."

His level gaze held a warning. "That's the worst time. When the victims feel the safest."

Annabelle wondered, looking at his threatening gaze, if he was a protector or a villain. At least he gave a warning. But on second thought, anyone who saved a crippled dog couldn't be all bad.

Symon looked up at Lizzie. "Another time."

Lizzie nodded. "So you're…going to be the caretaker now?"

"No," he said, "just his son."

"We're…discussing things. About the property, and all," Annabelle said.

"Oh. Well. Okay. You know what you want or you want to look at the menu?"

Annabelle knew what Wesley would have done. He would have looked over at her with a warm, or a sly, look as if to say she was what he wanted. But Wesley was her boyfriend, soon to be her fiancé, and then her husband.

"The menu," Symon said, reaching for it and beginning to look it over.

Annabelle saw Lizzie's questioning eyes.

Annabelle returned the look with a slight roll of her eyes as if to say she didn't know what to say. As if to say, *Why is this difficult?*

But of course it was.

Annabelle was promised to Wesley and here she was with another man. But she wasn't really with him. He was not another man. He was the caretaker's son and did that make him less of a man than Wesley? The law firm didn't do much for Aunt B's lawn. Didn't do anything, in fact.

Lizzie mouthed, "Married or…anything?"

Annabelle shrugged.

Symon looked over at her. She asked, "Are you married… or anything?"

"Not—" he grinned "—anything." He smiled at Lizzie, who smiled back.

As soon as Lizzie left them with the menus, Annabelle said, "Sorry, I didn't do too well in introducing you. My words don't seem to be working today."

"Don't worry about it," he said. "I have a thesaurus you can borrow."

Thesaurus? Was he some kind of editor with that publishing company he worked for?

They looked at the menu and Annabelle didn't know what she wanted but finally said, "I'll just have the salad."

Lizzie returned for their order.

"Southern fried catfish," Symon said and licked those firm, wide lips. "Haven't had that in a long time. And the fries and coleslaw. The lady will have the Pirate's Cave salad. You did say everything on it?" he asked. "Even onions?"

"I did."

"Good," he said. "Then we can share and each have a great dinner."

Annabelle pursed her lower lip, but a few bites of greasy fried catfish did have an appetizing ring to it.

Wide-eyed Lizzie took the menus. Annabelle looked around as if she wasn't familiar with the place. She supposed they should talk business. "I have a few questions," she said. "Since you're living on the property."

"Just a minute," he said. "The way I see it, I'm doing you a favor by taking care of the property and you're doing me a favor by letting me stay in the cottage that Miss B has already said I could stay in. That makes us close to equal, I'd say. So—" He spread his hands. "Shouldn't you answer my question first?"

Close to equal? What did that mean? Forty-nine and fifty-one percent? Then which one would he consider the fifty-one?

Well…sure…in a sense. But she shouldn't be there with a fellow with whom she was on an equal basis, should she? But no, even if Aunt B offered him the cottage and seemed fine with his staying there, it was still Aunt B's property and her cottage. But he was just being…what? Conversational?

Yes.

But she didn't know what to think of him. So, she should be…conversational.

And she knew to what question he referred. Through the years she learned how to answer when asked, "What do you do?"

She had a feeling he knew more about her than she knew about him. After all, he grew up at Aunt B's. He came to see her. She was glad, wanted him to stay.

Strange reaction from Aunt B.

Strange reaction from herself. She had a feeling he'd have that amused look if she said what she did. But was it amused? Maybe it was an inner sneer? Caretaker's sons probably thought less of society folks than society folks thought of them. Lizzie hadn't remembered his name, but knew him as the caretaker's son who'd been on a swim team.

And who had she and Lizzie been to him, if anyone?

"What do I do?" she said, repeating the question he'd asked. Then she gazed into his eyes. Why not be honest? Okay, she would. So she took a breath and said what she wouldn't dare say to anyone else. "I look pretty."

He stared, as if evaluating whether that was true. By now, any other man would already have commented on her looks. Why hadn't he? Because he knew it didn't really matter? Or… because he was only a caretaker's son who knew his place?

"Professionally?" he asked.

She nodded. "I—I have a rhinestone tiara to prove it."

His laughter didn't sound like amusement. It sounded like pleasure. So she laughed, too, thinking hers sounded like insecurity.

For the first time since he'd arrived, she thought he might like her.

A little.

Not that it mattered.

"You want to tell me about it?" he asked.

"About what?"

"Your career."

Did she?

"Maybe later," she said.

He looked pleased, then serious. Then he said, "You and I have something in common."

"What?" She thought she'd beat him to it. "Looking pretty?"

His laugh sounded genuine. "That, too, but please—" he held up his hands "—let's keep it between you and me." He took a sip of water, then said seriously, "The house-sitting. When I first went to New York, besides working with the publishing company, I began house-sitting. Got paid to stay in some fine places. That helped pay my own rent and was good research for my stories."

Annabelle listened with interest. His ideas on how to live as well as he did were as innovative as his ideas on how to take care of landscaping. She liked hearing about the places where he'd house-sat. And now, he wasn't getting paid to stay in the cottage, but he was getting it rent free. Very innovative, this guy.

She was intent upon his descriptions of places when Lizzie set their food before them. Annabelle closed her eyes for a moment and said a brief thanks. Opening them, she saw he was still but didn't know if he'd closed his eyes or said a prayer or not. Of course one didn't have to close the eyes. And he hadn't gone ahead and started eating.

He cut a piece of catfish and put it on her plate. She scraped some salad onto his. And so they shared a few bites of what each had ordered, ate, and talked about Savannah, and she forgot about Lizzie until they got up to leave and she noticed Lizzie's eyes seemed to have widened even more, still questioning.

Annabelle had no idea how to answer. In fact, she wasn't even sure of the question.

Chapter 9

After returning to Miss B's house, Annabelle invited Symon to sit in a rocker, but he felt more comfortable on the porch, leaned back against the post, one foot on the porch, the other on a step. That had been his place.

In New York, if he happened to be at a gathering where he wasn't recognized, he was immediately known and admired as soon as his pen name or book titles were mentioned. But he wasn't here to be admired as a writer.

Now was the time to find out if he could recapture that bond between him and Miss B. Have that sense of family he'd felt as a child and as a young person. He had succeeded professionally. Now, what about personally?

He didn't consider himself modest, but he was here not on a professional basis but on a personal quest to acknowledge Miss B as the most important influence in his life.

He wasn't here to add anyone to his fan club. He had stated the simple truth: that he wrote novels. And he had no reason to add that they were being looked at by a production company. Being looked at meant only a possibility of production, not a done deal, anyway.

He needed to keep his purpose in focus. If he was with a beautiful girl in New York, he'd be thinking of what was in it for him. Here, his purpose was to acknowledge and respect what Miss B had been to him.

Glancing at the flower bed, he smiled, thinking that Miss Annabelle reminded him of the pansy that had survived in spite of the weeds. He'd been careful not to disturb its roots and in just one day it had bloomed even more beautifully.

Yes, a way to show respect to Miss B would be for him to respect her niece even more than the landscape.

Of course, he couldn't be family. But surely they could at least be friends. He had not returned to get interested in a girl—and certainly not Miss B's niece. Even if the idea should ever strike him, he'd remind himself she was already spoken for and not his type anyway, having been a snobbish, sassy little girl.

She wasn't exactly that now, but that was beside the point and he didn't need to be trying to analyze her.

"I remember the first time I ever sat here," he said. "I was five years old."

"When she told you about the myth? After you lied?"

He nodded.

Annabelle scoffed, "What kind of lie could you tell at age five?"

"A big one." As the sun sank into the horizon and the shadows crept across the lawn and porch, he relived that childhood and the beginning of what would become his purpose in life. Thanks to Miss B. He thought of the stories he'd told in the past few years at writers' seminars about how Miss B had turned an active mind into a professional storyteller.

But while telling the stories to an attentive Annabelle, he didn't feel like a professional promoting his work to aspiring writers, but felt as if he were that little boy again. He was back in the mode of twenty-four years ago when Miss B had made him sit on the front porch and drink a glass of the sweetest iced tea he'd ever tasted.

Another woman, as dark as his daddy's coffee and wearing a dress the same color with a white apron over it, had served the tea on a silver platter. The glass sat on a little white thing that he learned later was a doily. It looked like a fancy cookie to him. It didn't feel like a cookie so he held it until Miss B took hers and placed it on her lap like a napkin. So he reckoned it was not a cookie and wouldn't try to eat it unless she did.

The dark woman went back inside, leaving him alone with Miss B, who sat with her feet firmly planted close together in the kind of shoes his daddy said he didn't know how women walked in. Miss B didn't say a word, didn't even rock the chair she sat in. He expected he was in trouble for telling a lie.

That's when she'd asked him if he knew how Savannah got its name.

He studied her, not sure what to say. Was she trying to trick him and make him tell another lie? He was scared of her because she lived in the big house and was rich, and he knew people with money could do anything. His daddy said she could make him lose his job and they'd end up in the Poor House. He didn't know what that was, but it didn't sound good.

His eyes felt stuck, looking at Miss B while she talked about myth and Save-Anna. His hands got cold so he eased his iced tea glass over on the step below him. It fell over and tea spilled all over the step.

Then she had that stuck look in her eyes. "What happened?" Miss B asked as she looked at the tea running over the step.

"It fell over. The ice was too heavy on one side."

She reached over to the table beside her and picked up a little bell and rang it. "Will-a-mean-uh." The brown woman in the white apron came to the screen door. "Fix this boy another glass of iced tea."

Miss B leaned her head back and kept her eyes closed for so long he wondered if she went to sleep. Then she stirred at the familiar screeching of the screen door as Will-a-mean-uh brought him a fresh glass of sweet tea. He handed her the empty glass. He held the second one with both hands and looked down at the step. His daddy always said, *Learn from your mistakes, boy.* He'd better not set the glass down there again. He set it on the porch and used a finger to stir the ice so Miss B would think it wasn't heavy on one side.

"All right," she said. "While you're drinking your tea, I want you to think about two things. One, think about that glass of tea falling over. And two, think about that broken slat in the picket fence. Think the strangest things you can about the tea and the slat, then tell me the stories. After that, tell me what really happened. Understand?"

"Yes, ma'am."

He could've told her the real story right then because when he'd climbed over that picket fence and his foot got caught between the slats, he heard it crack. The story he told her before was about the huge jackrabbit. Bigger than his own daddy. In the story Symon had run at the jackrabbit with his fingers out like claws and his face scrunched up, and that jackrabbit got so scared it tried to jump the fence and got its foot caught and he'd had to rescue it. It hopped away on one foot while it held the other one.

He waited because he liked sitting there with Miss B. She acted like he was in school, and she was teaching him something. He drank his tea while she rocked and waited. After a while he set his glass down real careful. "I'm ready. Can I tell the true ones first? They're not as good."

"Yes, that would be fine."

He took a deep breath. "I set the glass too close to the edge and it flipped over." He didn't think school could be any harder than this. He'd rather tell a lie any day. "The jackrabbit didn't get its foot caught in the fence. I did."

"Thank you for the truth." She didn't look mad, but that fence back there was still broke, and she knew it. "Now your pretend stories."

He liked that part. "I set my glass down and this thing slithered across my hand and I moved it real quick because a big ol' copperhead was crawling in that glass so I turned it over so it could get to it quicker."

Her eyes got bigger and bluer so he leaned toward her a little. He made his voice sound low as he could and scary. He moved his hands in a crawly way like a big copperhead would do. "After that copperhead slurped all the tea it started swallowing the ice."

He moved his twisting hands over his chest and his stomach and made his eyes bulge. "That froze its insides and it crawled back under the porch."

Waiting, he watched her looking like that was the greatest story she'd ever heard and she couldn't wait for the end.

He made her wait. After a long, scary minute he opened his mouth and grimaced. "Then it puked its guts out."

Her lips did a funny little movement and she put her finger to her lips. He thought she liked his story.

She cleared her throat. Probably, she was thinking about the copperhead's guts coming out its throat. "Now," she said, "the fence."

He reckoned she hadn't liked the jackrabbit one too much because when he told it before, she made him come sit on the porch. He'd try another one. It was a short one and he didn't like it as much as the jackrabbit one. "The caretaker got drunk and ran into it with the lawnmower."

He didn't know if she liked that one. Her breath came out heavy. "Do you think he learned his lesson and quit drinking on the job?"

"No, ma'am. He just fixed the fence."

She studied on it for a minute with a finger and a thumb touching her lips. She put her hand back down on her lap. "Well, it's always nice to have a good ending." Her eyes slid his way. "When you can."

The sun went behind a cloud. She stood up. "You run along home."

Knowing what he was supposed to do when a lady came into a room or stood, he jumped to his feet. "You gonna tell my daddy what I did?"

"We don't need to say a word about the tea. That was an accident." Her kind blue eyes turned serious. "Now, about the fence. Have you been told not to climb over that fence?"

Telling stories was easier, but she was standing and didn't want to hear any more. "Yes, ma'am."

"Then you just tell your daddy to get a new slat and fix the fence, that's all. And some white paint. Then tomorrow, your punishment will be to paint that slat."

He closed his eyes real tight, trying to look like that punishment would hurt worse than a hickory stick, or even worse than his daddy's whack. But he was so excited he could hardly wait. He bolted down the steps. "Bye. I gotta go tell Daddy."

Hearing the pleasing sound of light laugher from Annabelle, Symon returned his focus on the present, and the debt of gratitude he owed Miss B.

"She taught me that it was all right to make up stories and write them down. Then they wouldn't be lies. When she saw that I began to do that, at first in drawings until I learned to write, she had my daddy buy the best little cherry tree he could find, then she and I planted it together. She told me about George Washington not being able to tell a lie. She taught me to tell the truth. And when I made up a story, no matter how bad, it was to have a good ending. Good always had to win over the bad." He laughed. "Then it became a contest. Who grew faster, me or the cherry tree."

"Oh, that's wonderful," Annabelle said. "I had no idea

you and Aunt B had that kind of relationship. You have a lot of stories like that?"

"Well, let's see," he mused, "how many days are there in about eighteen years? I'd say I'd have at least half that many stories. I'd like to put them into a book. Write about her. She was a dominating factor in my life."

"Mine, too," she said. "I wasn't with her a lot when I was growing up, but each time was a special occasion. She always taught me something. But not by lecturing like my parents did. I'm beginning to understand why you want to write about her."

"What about that book you mentioned? You said you'd tell me later about your profession." He looked out at the sky and lawn. The moon had risen in the light gray sky. A ball of yellow butter, softening the shadows, spreading over the porch, and over Annabelle as if she were warm toast. There could be something mesmerizing about moonlight, and a pretty girl.

She looked away from him and out into the twilight, reminding him of her reaction after her rhinestone tiara comments. She'd given a short laugh and a shrug of one pretty shoulder and looked away as if the subject were over and she shouldn't have said it in the first place.

He detected a vulnerability about her that he hadn't seen when she was a child. But then, maybe even now, he had his prejudices—or was it sensitivity about those living the good life while he and his dad worked for them?

He watched her swallow, moisten her lips, take a deep breath and begin telling him about her pretty life.

"I loved it," she said. "The dressing up, the acting like a big girl, competing, winning, feeling pretty, taking lessons in piano, singing, dancing to see where my talent lay."

"Where was that?"

Her laugh sounded thin. "My mama said my talent was just being pretty. But I could learn to play the piano and sing enough to enter contests. So…" She spoke rather self-consciously. "I don't really have a talent."

"I see," he said. "Then I suppose your book would be about the girl who succeeded without a talent."

"No. The title would be *Pretty Is as Pretty Does*."

He stared at her. A memory was beginning to emerge like a fish heading toward the bait, and then comprehension bit. "Willamina," he breathed.

She nodded. "I was about five years old."

"I would have been ten."

"I stuck my tongue out at you in the kitchen."

"And Willamina said that was not pretty."

Annabelle was nodding. "She said pretty is as pretty does."

"So that's what others want you to write about?"

She uncrossed her ankles and her feet moved as if they were thinking of going somewhere. Her voice lowered. "Celeste, the modeling agency director, wants me to write what I teach at the studio. Makeup, etiquette, poise, posture for children and teens. She says it would sell particularly well in studios and for those in pageants or thinking about entering them."

He agreed. "Sounds like a possibility."

"I know," she said. "Women, girls, even guys, want to make a good appearance, improve themselves. But I'd want to take it further. You see." She cleared her throat and her hand grasped the arm of the rocker. "I speak to church groups, at schools, at modeling shows. But I have to downplay the pretty part. It's assumed that I'm stuck on myself. I have to say that there are all kinds of gifts and my looks are what God gave me, and winning a beauty pageant paid my way into college."

She must have noticed his surprise.

"I really did pay my way," she said. "Because I wanted to. But, if I were to write anything I'd want to include faith and talk about inner beauty. You know, like having Jesus in one's heart. That's more important than just looking good.

My agency director doesn't want that included. Says it's an entirely different subject." She laughed lightly. "I don't know why I told you all that."

"Maybe because I have connections with a publishing company," he said, noticing already her mouth was open and she began to shake her head. He grinned. "Everybody wants to write a book, you know."

"No, I didn't even think about that."

He shrugged. "Well, maybe it's because I'm easy to talk to."

She put her hands on her lap and looked at them and rocked gently.

But he thought he knew why she'd opened up to him. He was safe. He was the caretaker's son. She could be honest. She had no need to try and impress him.

And…okay. She had a fiancé. And she had Christian morals. And the biggest consideration at this juncture in his endeavors was that she was Miss B's niece.

Probably time for him to return to the cottage and get on with his purpose. After all, he had a public to please.

Punctuating that thought, as he rose from where he sat a sleek sand-colored sedan came up the drive and Annabelle said, "Oh, there's Wes."

Symon watched as the car door slammed and the fellow in dress pants and a white shirt and tie hurried along the brick walkway. Wes slowed with surprise on his face when he saw Symon, and his questioning glance went quickly from Symon to Annabelle.

She walked over and introduced them as Wesley Powers-Lippincott and Symon Sinclair, who was a friend of Miss B and staying in the cottage.

Symon extended his hand. "Nice to meet you, Wesley," which Wesley reciprocated with, "You, too."

Wesley, who was less than remarkable looking in Symon's estimation, walked up the steps and put his arm around Annabelle's waist. "Sorry to be so late." He had light brown curly hair conservatively cut, maybe even a little thin at the hair line. He looked pleasant, kind of like one of Symon's characters whom you wouldn't expect would hurt a fly, but who, like SweetiePie, really had a rotten heart and would swat one at less than a moment's notice.

"I'm just leaving," Symon said, and lifted his hand as he walked down the steps.

"Thanks, Symon," Annabelle said.

"You bet." He walked on, having no idea what she was thanking him for.

For leaving?

When he reached the driveway and veered off toward the cottage, he turned his head to the left and saw Annabelle step back from Wesley as if they'd just broken away from a kiss or embrace.

Then her hands were gesturing as if she were in animated conversation.

Maybe reprimanding him for working late and causing her to take up with the caretaker's son?

He reached his car. Then he remembered. Her clothes were still in the back.

Chapter 10

As soon as the obligatory kiss ended, Wes still held on to her waist and said, "Who is that and why is hc in the cottage?"

"He's a friend of Aunt B, and he's doing some work on the property."

"Sinclair?" he mused. "Wasn't that the name of—?"

"The caretaker, yes. That's his son."

"Why was he sitting here with you?"

She stepped back and lifted her hands. "We were talking."

"About what?"

She huffed. "What difference does it make?"

He ducked his head slightly and gave her a look from his deep blue eyes that was normally endearing. "You're my girl," he said softly.

Not wanting an audience, she said, "Let's go inside."

As soon as they entered the foyer, she turned to him, and spoke in a monotone. "Wes, shouldn't we be talking about us? How was your day? Are you tired? Would you like something to eat? Drink?"

Before he could do more than stare at her, a knock sounded on the screen door. She and Wes turned. She stepped to the screen and opened it.

"You forgot your clothes," he said. "I thought you might need them."

"Yes, I—I will." She took the hanger and the bag from him. "Thank you."

"You're welcome. Good night."

She said, "Good night."

She glanced at Wes, whose eyes questioned. If he had a question, he could just ask it. She stepped past him and walked toward the staircase. "I'll take these up to my room."

He said to her retreating back, "I'll be in the kitchen. I think I would like something to drink."

"Diet Coke's in the fridge."

When she returned he was sitting at the small kitchen table beneath a window that had a moonlit view of the patio. He'd poured her a glass of Coke. She sat opposite him. He began to tell her briefly of his grueling day.

She knew he was waiting. Not angrily. He wouldn't yell at her. He wouldn't demand anything. He was level-headed, like a good attorney should be. He would listen to the evidence.

Maybe she'd like for him to be less level-headed at times. But there was no reason to be. They loved each other. They'd known for more than three years they were right for each other. Would marry. They'd do it right.

Their dating had been rather passionate at first. Then her parents had died, and her outlook on precarious life became more serious. In college she was preparing for, running for and then winning Miss Georgia Sunshine, homecoming queen and then first runner-up for Miss Georgia. She'd had to finish college. He finished first and went to law school. He did not want to be dependent on her trust fund or inheritance. She wanted to have a profession.

They were busy. She was speaking, and holding summer Bible studies for teens at church. She couldn't very well be promiscuous when telling teens not to be. And living with Megan and Lizzie, not to mention the high standards of Aunt B, her lifestyle had been pretty much fixed.

Nothing had changed. And she had nothing to feel guilty about. And frankly, there was no ring on her finger. But of course they'd talked that over, too. Why rush a ring when they were discussing Aunt B and her future, which would certainly involve them.

So when he finished with his boring account she told about hers, as boringly as she could. But she couldn't help but laugh again when repeating some of the stories Symon had told her.

Wes listened, smiled politely, nodded, agreed they were cute little stories. But she felt as if they were like some foods warmed over—not as tasty as when fresh. *Guess you had to be there.*

"Anyway," she said, "Aunt B asked me to be congenial with her guest. He's been away for a few years."

"That's nice of you, but you don't know him."

No, but last night, after turning out the light and looking out the window to see that car across the way, she'd felt safe and secure out here alone in this big house with that familiar stranger in the cottage. Just as Aunt B had said she'd felt when the caretaker had lived there. Annabelle had gone to sleep with a smile on her face.

Another thought occurred to her. "Wes, did I know you when I first went out with you?"

"You knew my family. My background."

"I know his, too."

"Yeah. That's my point. You know…"

"Know what, Wes?"

"Come on, Annabelle. You remember Aunt B's refusing

to fire his dad even after he was too sick to work. Everybody knows his dad drank himself to death."

"So you're judging Symon for what his dad did?"

Wesley's eyes closed. His lips became taut. He shook his head.

She kept on. "Aunt B said his dad was the best landscaper around. And he didn't drink on the job until his pain worsened. She judged him by his good qualities, not his worst ones. And if you happen to notice, he's been doing what his dad did. Don't the yard and flower beds look much better?"

Wesley sighed heavily. "Frankly, I didn't notice."

"Wes, I have contact with men all the time. All kinds. And you know some come on to me. We've talked about that. Why, all of a sudden, do you care about this one?"

He spread his hands in a helpless gesture. "I don't know. I guess because I've been caught up in a case all week, and tonight I had to work late. I hurried as much as I could, then I got here and saw him sitting there like he owned the place. He has an air about him."

Annabelle thought about that. Wes was right. Symon hadn't displayed any sense of guilt or inhibition about being there with her when Wes came. And of course, he shouldn't have. He wasn't guilty of anything. And the air about him? She'd noticed it. It was as if he was his own person and anyone else's opinion just might not make a lot of difference to him. She didn't see that as a detriment.

"I'm sorry," Wes said. "I sound like a pompous cad. I know with my head that knowing someone's family and having a supposedly good background is not a person's worth. I know that, Annabelle. I believe it. And yet, this slipped out. I think...I hope...I'm just jealous you had a great evening with a guy. I'm glad you did. But I also wish it had been with me."

"We can't do this, Wesley. Have you be jealous when I

speak to another guy. I mean, you spend time with female paralegals, clients, secretaries, lawyers, judges. I don't intend to go there."

"I know. I'm sorry."

She nodded. "When we were walking to River Street, I was wishing you were with us."

She braced herself for another comment from Wes. But he didn't seem to notice. She should have said she wished he were there instead of Symon, not along with them. But she had enjoyed the afternoon and evening. Symon was... interesting.

Wes said, "Maybe I should befriend him. He's new in town. Been gone awhile."

"That would be nice." She knew Wesley was trying to prove he was neither prejudiced nor jealous. She laughed lightly. "But when would you have time? You gotta befriend me."

Grinning, he rose from the chair and came over to her. "I love you, Annabelle."

She stood and went into his open arms.

Even then, she wondered if they were being watched. As if it mattered. Well, yes, maybe it did. She was Wesley's girl. Everyone knew that. Everyone should know it.

There's nothing wrong with being friendly to a friend of Aunt B. And why was she even thinking about it? She shouldn't. So she wouldn't. She raised her face to Wesley and their lips met. That felt good. Like it should.

"Hey," he said after a long moment. "Maybe we'd better get that ring on your finger."

She even wondered about that. Did he say that because he didn't want to wait any longer? Or because she had talked to another guy?

"Maybe," she said. "But better than white gold circling my finger are real arms circling me."

So he put his arms around her again. Sometimes she just

didn't want him to let go, and she knew he felt the same way. That's when one of them would move away, honor the commitment they'd made to each other and the Lord. And heaven forbid they ever do anything improper in Aunt B's house. Not that she was considering it.

"You want popcorn with that Coke?"

He stepped back, lifted his arm and looked at his watch. "I could use a little relaxation. About time for the cops show. Want to watch it if it's not too late?"

She glanced at the wall clock. "Not even nine yet. Sure. Turn it on. I'll make popcorn."

He got their drinks and walked out.

She put a bag in the microwave and punched the buttons. Just as she reached for a bowl, her phone rang.

She winced, seeing the caller ID. Lizzie wouldn't call from work just to chat.

She punched the button. "Lizzie?"

"Symon's here," Lizzie said. It made Annabelle's emotions jump like the *pop-pop-pop* of the corn.

"Wha–what's he doing?"

Lizzie giggled. "Looking at the decorations. He'd like to take the tour. And…Annabelle…he asked if I'd like to talk with him after I get off work at ten. Is that okay with you?"

Annabelle looked at the doorway. "Why do you ask me, Lizzie? That's your business."

"Well, you were here with him."

"Just being nice to Aunt B's friend." She spoke low and was glad the corn was popping. "You silly. You know I'm engaged to Wes."

"Ha! You know how many times I expected to get married and didn't. And, we all know about a woman's prerogative."

"Well, mine's still intact. It's your decision. Okay?"

"Believe me, I'll turn on all the charm I have."

Annabelle laughed. "Don't worry, you have plenty. I mean, he got back to you in a hurry."

"Well." She sounded doubtful. "He said the pirate scene is research for a possible story idea. You're sure?"

"Of course. Have fun."

"Okay. Gotta go."

Why in the world would Lizzie think she needed her permission? Couldn't people be friends, or acquaintances, anymore? Wes appeared in the doorway. Annabelle laid the phone on the countertop. "That was Lizzie. Guess who just asked her out?"

He shrugged.

"Symon."

"Is she going?"

"Looking forward to it."

Wes looked pleased. "Sounds like the program's back on."

A few minutes later, she was aware of leaning against Wes's arm, sharing the popcorn, listening to his occasional comments about the program, his filling her in on what she'd missed, but she kept thinking about Symon and Lizzie together. Lizzie was concerned about everyone else having a close relationship with a guy, yet none of hers ever lasted very long. Guys either went away or she sent them away.

Somehow Annabelle didn't think Lizzie and Symon were right for each other. Lizzie seemed a little too desperate to find a guy. She bemoaned the fact that Megan and Michael were close and that Annabelle and Wesley would marry. Lizzie was fun and beautiful. But she could be too vulnerable to the charms of Symon Sinclair.

Charms?

Where in the world did that come from?

He hadn't done a single charming thing. It wasn't charm. It was…charisma? Well, for goodness' sake, she wasn't blind. And he was entertaining and somewhat an enigma.

She sighed and shrugged a shoulder.

"Yeah," Wesley said, reaching into the bowl for another handful of popcorn. "That was a little stupid, wasn't it?"

"Yes," she said, thinking he had to be talking about the TV program. "It really was."

Chapter 11

Monday morning dawned bright and clear. After Annabelle exercised, showered and dressed in shorts and a tank top, she went out onto the porch with her laptop. She knew Symon was working near the house, pruning, pulling, hoeing, pouring stuff from bags. The earthy smell was as pleasant as the soft breeze teasing the moss on the trees on the sunlit morning.

Her curiosity was getting the better of her, just as Sweetie-Pie's seemed to do when she jumped from windowsill to windowsill to watch either Mudd or Symon, or both.

When he came around front he said he'd had a nice conversation with Miss B over the weekend.

"How'd she get your number?"

"Landline in the cottage."

Annabelle chuckled. "She uses her cell but won't give up her landlines. We can exchange cell numbers if you like."

"Fine," he said. "And you can always call the cottage and leave a message. The last digit is a two instead of three like in the house."

She scoffed, "I wouldn't know what to tell you to do, anyway. You seem to be doing all right."

"Comes with experience." He gestured to the front bed. "These are just about ready. I need to order the plants."

"Would you like to use my car to haul them in? It's older and has more room."

His glance was quick. "I'll have them delivered."

"Did you ask Aunt B?"

"No."

"That will cost."

"Is that a problem?"

She shrugged. "No, but Aunt B is frugal. She's retired now, so she's careful."

"You want to pay for it?"

She opened her mouth ready to say no. But of course she would if that's what Aunt B wanted. "If it's not astronomical."

"Don't be concerned. The plants are the gift of an anonymous donor."

She lifted her hands. Nothing was in her control. "That's between you and Aunt B."

"Exactly," he affirmed and wiggled a finger at Mudd, who rose.

He must be finished for the time being. But she had to know. This was what she came out here for, so just as he turned away she called, "Did you have a nice weekend?" His car hadn't been there late Saturday evening when Wes brought her home. Nor on Sunday morning when Wes picked her up for church.

"Fine." He looked over his shoulder with that expression again. He seemed to know what was on her mind so she might as well say it. "How was your date with Lizzie?"

"Oh," he exclaimed and placed his hand on his forehead. "How can I find words?" He strode over to the steps and sat in his place against the post. After Mudd glanced around warily and decided he was safe from the cat on the front windowsill, he settled at the bottom of the steps.

Annabelle sighed heavily and parked herself in the rocker.

Symon grinned. "It wasn't a date. At least not the way you're implying. She invited me to take the tour. I took her up on it. It was information. But," he said quickly. "Right now I'm concentrating on where to live and the cherry tree project. Besides, she had plans to meet someone from a dating service on Saturday."

"Oh, not again. That girl's asking for trouble."

"I warned her." He paused. "But I did go out with her brother Saturday night."

Her expression must have been what made him chuckle. "Lizzie told him about me, so we met at the fitness center and swam awhile Saturday morning. And, let's see, I slept late Sunday morning. Miss B never let us work on Saturday or Sunday unless it was an emergency, so I took it easy most of the day."

"Do you have a special girl?" she asked.

"They're all special. But nothing serious. No commitments," he said and changed the subject by asking, "How was your weekend?"

"Fine. After my Saturday morning classes, Wes and I spent the weekend together. Most of it, anyway."

Instead of the usual going out to dinner followed by a movie or some event, she'd cooked a special meal for Wes at Aunt B's, a welcome break from all the salads she seemed to live on. Then they'd gone out to watch a movie both had been wanting to see. They'd gone to church Sunday, then had lunch with his parents.

"Was it that bad?" Symon said, interrupting her thoughts.

She laughed lightly. "No. Well, yes. That murder case is a big one for the firm, and for Wes's future. It's really weighing on him." She sighed. "I guess I'll just work on my book, which is just dull facts."

"Remember, tell the stories."

"I don't think like you. You're more entertaining than television."

"That's not saying much," he said, and she chuckled with him until he asked, "Why do you females wear all that makeup?"

He appeared serious so she said, "It's fun. And besides that, it's to enhance one's best attributes. Diminish the not so good."

He nodded. "Like I'm doing with the flower beds. It's a process."

"Oh. You exfoliated the beds?"

At his askance expression she laughed. "Maybe you don't, but we girls exfoliate our skin to remove the dead cells."

"Okay," he said. "That's the point. Relate the skin to a flower bed. Remove the weeds, have a clean slate, begin to enhance and eventually you have the results you want. Make that analogy. Draw a few flowers on the page and you intrigue your reader."

He made it sound simple.

"By the way." He squinted. "Are you exfoliated or enhanced?"

She slapped the arm of the rocker. "If you have to ask, I've failed."

He just raised his eyebrows, and removed himself from the porch. When he stood across from her on the other side of the banister he said, "Do you have plans for this afternoon?"

"I don't have my four o'clock class. The children are out of school today. When that happens, we don't hold the modeling classes. But I'm meeting with Celeste to plan the summer fashion show."

"I'm going in to order the flowers. If you want, we could take care of what we have to do and afterward we could go to a bookstore and I'll show you how to get ideas for your book."

She really hadn't felt confident about the book idea, but he made it sound like a doable project that could be worthwhile. And Celeste had begun to sound like it was not an option.

"In case you're wondering," he said, drawing her attention back to him, "Miss B is the closest thing I've had to a mom. So, let's see. That would make you and me, what? Cousins?"

Why in the world "kissing cousins" popped into her mind, or why her eyes went to his lips, she didn't know. *My goodness gracious,* she'd been around male models all her life, handsome men. In fact Wesley was very handsome. So there was nothing wrong in recognizing such a fact. That had been her first thought upon meeting Wesley. When she was introduced to him, he was all dressed up in dinner attire and she'd thought, *My, he's actually very handsome.* And he'd proved to be very kissable that very night.

That's exactly where her mind should be. On Wes. And she'd told herself this was the perfect time to concentrate on the book. Symon seemed willing and able to help.

If she said no, what would that indicate? That she didn't want to be friends with him? He'd already made friends with Lizzie and Paul. Come to think of it, she felt as if they were already friends. Had been from almost the time he'd sat there talking about his feelings for Aunt B. Besides that, she enjoyed him very much.

Wes wouldn't be particularly thrilled. But he had no reason for concern. And to prove it, she closed her laptop and stood.

"Sure," she said. "I'd like to be there by two."

Chapter 12

Symon ordered the plants and flowers from the garden center. Annabelle said she'd be in a back room of the department store, choosing clothes for the fashion show before they were put on the racks. But whoever finished first would wait for the other.

Approaching the store, he spied her near the front with two other women. She looked out and acknowledged him with a direct gaze and a smile, then returned her attention to the other women.

He knew which would be Celeste. The tall blonde with a sleek chignon, long legs in off-white pants, a jacket over a grass-green blouse and really high heels. The conservative-looking woman in a suit and white collared shirt would be the manager.

Of course he already knew how Annabelle looked from the moment she walked out of the house and got into his car.

"What's the color of your sweater set?" he'd asked. "I have

to describe women's clothes in my writing and am sorely lacking."

She gave him a look. "The color of the tank and cardigan is mist mélange." Her cranberry-colored lips were all the color she needed. Then there was the big round goldish jewelry, bronze maybe.

He doubted his characters would wear mist mélange. Well, unless they were models.

Annabelle's knees were quite attractive, too, below her straight ivory skirt—well, straight as could be…considering.

Wearing slacks and a short-sleeved sport shirt, he felt a mite overdressed for the garden center but maybe passable for the lovely lady. Would she care that he wrote successful books under a pen name? But what would be the point? They were relating well just the way things were. He reminded himself he was here to impress Miss B, if anyone, and the trip to the bookstore was for her niece.

Annabelle and the blonde exited the store. The blonde walked on down the corridor and every head turned. She looked to be maybe in her forties. But everything about her said style and beauty.

"Ahem," Annabelle said, and he looked at her as if he hadn't known she'd walked up to him. She darted a sly glance down the corridor and said with a smug smile, "That's Celeste."

"I figured," he said, then grinned. "Get things settled?"

"The beginning. Chose some really nice fashions. Next is getting the children and teens and trying them on and practicing for the show. Ever tried to get a six-year-old to stand straight, walk gracefully, pivot instead of turn, smile even if she trips on the runway, but don't trip. And not flap her arms like she's flying?"

"I'll stick with still life," he said as they began to walk toward the bookstore.

The first thing he did upon entering was go straight to

first table and pick up a book and stick his nose into it. "Ah, heaven." He inhaled deeply. "I love the smell of books."

Her nose wrinkled. "Dirt, fertilizer and now books."

"Try it." He shoved it toward her.

She sniffed. "Definitely dead trees. Not bad, but I kind of like lipstick. Right under my nose, you know."

He forced his eyes not to linger on the luscious-looking lips she moistened with her tongue. They were parted in a faint smile. Maybe waiting for a comment or compliment? Best not to go there. So he laid the book down and shook his head. "Not even a close second to dirt."

His eyes naturally went to the shelf marked bestselling novels. Two of his were there, still on the list. As he led her down the aisle, he saw three of his older ones on a shelf facing them.

"Aunt B reads a lot," she said, walking along beside him. "I sometimes read a little before I go to sleep. Romances or women's fiction. I don't stay up late. Have to get my beau—" She grimaced, looking up at him and said, "My rest."

He just shook his head, wondering why she had such trouble about looking beautiful. He took her elbow and steered her into the nonfiction section. "Okay, let's look for subjects that go along with what you do. Beauty? Nutrition? Modeling?

"These are helpful in seeing how things are put together. They look like what Celeste wants me to do." She shrugged. "Now I need to get faith into it."

He wasn't sure he was the one to tell her about that, but he'd try. "You have a good start with your title. When you told me you wanted faith in the book, that said a lot about you."

She seemed to consider that.

"You could write in an introduction or beneath your picture what you believe. You don't have to preach a sermon. Tell your little stories and make a point of what you learned, like Willamina saying pretty is as pretty does."

She smiled at him as if he'd given her a present and breathed, "Why didn't I think of that?"

"It's not your talent," he said blandly, as if he was not delighted at pleasing her. And her grin meant she knew he was being playful.

She picked out a few books and they'd almost reached the front when she stopped. "Oh, she said. "Are your books in here?"

He had to think quick. Didn't seem the time or way to bring it up, while she was being so uncertain about hers. He could say something truthful. "I sent Miss B each one. She probably has them."

"Wonder why she never mentioned them." Then she shrugged and smiled. "Maybe because I haven't been around that much. I've had my busy life."

He tried to make light of it. "Just another book in her massive collection." His books were called thrillers. But to some they might mean no more than blood and gore and mayhem committed by killers.

While Annabelle paid for her books, the manager kept glancing at him, as if she wanted to speak. He walked around a bookshelf, away from her searching eyes.

After they left the store, Annabelle said, "Looks like I had competition in there. She kept staring at you."

He jested,. "Probably because I'm so pretty."

"Oh." She stuck a finger in her open mouth and made a gagging sound, then quickly looked around as if someone else might be looking.

He motioned toward an exit they could take. "If I'd known we were competing, I would have exfoliated." Her quick laughter started, then stopped when he asked, "Females usually stare at you?"

She winced. "I must sound so stuck on myself. I was trying to joke about her staring at you. You see…" She continued as they walked to the parking lot. "Parents of the children in my class recognize me. And I speak at churches, and sing. Also at mother-daughter banquets, so I'm recognized."

"Does that bother you?"

"Not when they say they heard me speak and my message meant something. Maybe helped their children see that respect for parents is important. But not when they gush about my looks."

"But that's your talent, your profession. Just as Wesley must dress the part of a successful attorney. A judge wears a robe. Miss B looked the part of a conservative teacher."

"I know." She sighed. "I'm just feeling insecure lately."

"I have a cure for that," he said as they headed toward the car.

"What?"

"I'll tell you in due time."

She gave him her *whatever* glance, and after getting into the car, she looked through the books again and made comments.

When they arrived at Miss B's the delivery truck pulled in behind them. After the plants were set out and the truck left, Annabelle came out onto the porch. "Okay," he said, "Time to get rid of those insecurities." He drew an invisible line over the plants with his finger.

"You want me to do that?"

He was astounded. "Have you never planted a flower?"

"I've picked them. Does that count?"

"Nope. You can use the experience in your book. How it feels to get your hands in the earth. To smell it up close. To feel one with the dirt. To be mesmerized by the smell of earth and fertilizer."

"Fertilizer? What's it made of?"

"Don't ask," he said. "Put on some old clothes and help."

"Old clothes?" Then her laughter bubbled out. "Gotcha!"

He turned and headed for the cottage. "I'll get my work clothes on."

He returned before she did and began setting plants near where each should be planted. Soon she came out wearing a holey pair of jeans. He figured they were from the time when holey was the style. And she wore a T-shirt that had seen better days.

"Found these in a kitchen drawer," she said, tugging on rubber gloves that reached to her elbows. Then she turned and posed as if on a runway.

"Perfect," he approved. "You look downright sloppy."

"Thanks," she replied, "but I need to work in the shade so I don't end up striped."

"You have a bias against a farmer's tan," he teased.

"Well, excuse me," she sassed. "My purpose in life has been to smile, look pretty, please everyone and never get dirty."

They got the tools and brought them up. He planted the shrubs where he'd taken out any damaged ones and she scooped out the holes for the small plants and flowers.

They planted. He'd yell at her occasionally when she started to put a pink bloom where he wanted a white one, then he'd apologize and she'd laugh.

And at times he'd watch her dig, even move a wiggly worm to a safe place with her gloved fingers, tenderly place a little flower in the hole, fill it and then pat the dirt as if consoling it. His thoughts drifted to his reason for coming here. Finding a place to settle, maybe relating to Miss B like family. He hadn't even considered relating to her niece. He needed to stay focused.

"Enough," he said after a while. "We can leave the rest for me to do in the morning."

"Can I help again?"

"What?" He pretended chagrin. "You still have insecurities, after all this?"

She shrugged. "I don't know. Haven't thought about it for the past hour."

He didn't know if she'd stop smiling, so he did and asked, "What's for supper?"

Without hesitation, she said, "I make a mean salad," and at his sneer, added, "and a delicious peanut butter and jelly sandwich."

"A guy could get cleaned up for that."

And a while later they sat in Miss B's kitchen. While they ate, she said, "You did that on purpose, didn't you? Had me work in the flower bed?"

He laid his sandwich down and talked over his peanut butter. "I didn't force you."

She smiled. "I'm not complaining. It's good to do something and not think. But I've concluded that writing the book would be like closure on one part of my life, and then I can feel all right about doing something else."

He waited, while she washed down a bite with water. Then she said, "I don't think I want to compete in pageants anymore. If I didn't win I'd be a loser. If I won, I'd soon be a former again. I'm always introduced as the former something. As if everything is in the past."

"It's an accomplishment. Be proud of it."

"I am. But I want to feel I'm doing something now. Do you understand that?"

"I sure do," he said. "Maybe like my swimming. I loved the competition, the awards, the attention. But the day came when it was over. I could have become a coach."

She nodded. "Like I became an instructor at the modeling studio."

"Nothing wrong with either. But my choice was not to be a coach, but a writer. What do you want?"

"Be a teacher like Aunt B. Settle down. Be a wife and mother."

She sounded to him like someone ready to settle down. Surely she'd told Wesley that. And surely Wesley wouldn't hesitate. "Then…why don't you?"

She sat for a moment, thoughtful. "Well, it's like that flower bed. You can't make it look right and plant the flowers until you get the weeds out. See, you're making me think like you."

He just hoped he could keep his thoughts on the straight and narrow. He liked the fact she confided in him, wanted his advice. He hoped he had some wisdom and could impart it. "Don't forget," he said. "Weeds reappear. It's constant work. Flower beds, and life, are never free of weeds." He looked pointedly at her. "But you wouldn't appreciate the beauty of the flowers if you hadn't seen the weeds."

"Oh," she said as if delighted. "That sounds profound. I'll have to put that in my little book."

He scoffed, "I probably got it from one of mine."

She jumped up. "I'm going to see if your books are in the library." Soon she returned, shaking her head. "The only Sinclair book in there has the first name of Upton."

He thought that rather funny. When she saw that he was laughing, her sympathetic expression changed and she laughed, too.

Annabelle longed to be thought of as more than Miss Sunshine.

Wasn't that sort of like him being known as Sy DeBerry?

He liked their relating simply as Annabelle and Symon.

She had a lot of inner qualities. And he thought she had a lot more flowers in her garden than weeds.

Could he say the same for himself?

Chapter 13

Symon kept reminding himself he was not a little boy anymore. He was a man now. He and Miss B could relate as mature adults.

They had, on the phone. But he heard and felt the uncertainty in both their voices.

As he worked the property, mowed around the cherry tree, kept seeing it demolished, remembering it as it had been through the years, he wasn't so certain what was fact or fiction.

He'd seen her only once since he left for New York, when he returned to give her his first book. Her brother and his wife were having a dinner party at the house that night. He hadn't come in. She hadn't invited him in. She'd hugged him, thanked him, and he'd left. Never returned.

Until now.

Other than that, it had been four years. After college he worked on the estate during the summer. His dad's health was failing and Symon did most of the work. After getting the property ready for fall, one pleasant evening while Miss B sat on the porch in her rocker, he walked up.

"I'll be leaving soon for New York," he said, standing on the top step and bracing his hand against the post where he had leaned his back for so many years.

Her breath caught. "You know anyone there? Have a place to stay? I know some people—"

"No," he said quickly. He'd resolved he would not be dependent on anyone. He would live his life by his rules and in his own way, taking from another person only what he worked for.

"I have an agent," he said. "I will be in his guest house until I approve possible lodging."

"He...likes your book."

She seemed delighted. He felt that way, too, tried to hide it but couldn't. He felt kind of like he'd felt when he'd finally gotten to paint a slat in the picket fence. And when he was twelve and he'd come to say his daddy would teach him to drive the mower if she approved.

She'd lifted her chin in that teacherly way of hers. "Is that what you plan to do with your life, Symon? Have you forgotten your goal of putting those stories on paper. You going to get your joy on that big machine?"

"Well, yes, ma'am," he said. "My daddy will teach me everything about that machine. He's already been teaching me about starting and stopping. Now, if I don't experience it, how is my killer going to learn to fix the brakes on that contraption so the murder looks like an accident?"

She nodded and said quietly, "You do have a point."

He'd felt it, the deep breath that swelled his chest. He'd closed his hands like he had to do something to keep from running up and hugging her. And he thought she did, too. She reached out and held on to the banister. He had to keep his distance. She was the teacher, the employer. He was the caretaker's son.

As time moved on, and he grew from child to growing boy, to teenager, she'd said, "I think it's time you learned to drive my town car."

He'd been confident enough by then to say, "I'm not wearing one of those jackets and caps with a brim and scrambled eggs on it."

"Fine. A white shirt and nice pants will do." She laughed and said, "No shorts."

He scoffed playfully, "What about a bathing suit? After all, I made the swim team."

"Oh, Symon. That's wonderful. I guess all that swimming in the creek paid off. Even if you did do it against my better judgment."

"Where I swam was like a deep pool. And going upstream like a salmon may have its advantages." He laughed, then became serious. "The coach says I'm a natural. Which means he wants me to practice more."

"You want that?"

"Yes, ma'am. If I do well on the team I could get a scholarship to college. Besides," he said, since he knew she delighted in his stories, "I already have this idea about a guy with extrasensory powers who looked into the mind of a swimmer he's jealous of and gives him a brain hemorrhage. Want to hear more?"

"Write it down. I'll read it when you make it into a book."

"Thank you," he said.

"You're welcome," she said and for Christmas she gave him a year's paid membership at the fitness club.

That had worked well for him through high school, then college. And then he went off to New York.

When he'd talked to her on the phone and told her he was writing a book about her influence in his life and writing, her uncertainty reminded him of how his publisher had reacted when he told him.

Jim had pursed his lips for a moment. "You don't mean

change genres. No, you know better than that." He leaned forward, propped his forearms on the desk for a thoughtful moment. "You mean like Grisham writing that Christmas book and Patterson with his children's books."

Then Symon saw the light come into the publisher's eyes like it had through the years when he'd told Miss B his story ideas. Jim began to nod. "Your speaking engagements always result in additional sales. They love your childhood stories. Your audiences always want to know more about what sparked ideas for you."

He was nodding. "Yes, it may be time for your own story. Young author makes good. Most writers become overnight successes after twenty or thirty years. You did it at the beginning."

Symon shrugged a shoulder and accepted that. He'd done it with his first submitted book. But his writing had begun when he was five years old sitting on the porch while Miss B told about save-Anna.

Then Jim laughed. "This is perfect. A thriller mystery writer with a book titled *The Cherry Tree*. They'll love it. The title is so bland, so common, everyone will want to know what's in it. Only interest anyone has in a cherry tree, other than springtime in our nation's capital, is George Washington. Cannot tell a lie."

Symon stared.

Jim stopped laughing and began to nod. "You said something about that in a talk you gave. About fiction not being a lie, but truth in living color." He began to nod. "Your cherry tree comes in there somewhere." He leaned back. "Okay. Write it."

Yes, Symon thought then. And now.

The subtitle would be, *Where the Truth Lies*.

That's why he'd come back. To find out just what he and Miss B were to each other.

So much depended on how she chose to relate to him.

Would she want him to sit in her parlor and drink tea or coffee and look at the photo albums? Or would he sit on the porch, propped against that long white column?

She would decide if he'd relate to her as Sy DeBerry, acclaimed thriller novelist.

Or…Symon DeBerry Sinclair, the caretaker's son.

Chapter 14

Annabelle had just finished on the treadmill when Symon called to say the porch repairmen would be there shortly. She hurriedly showered, dressed and settled at the breakfast table with a bagel, cream cheese, orange juice and her laptop.

"Scat," she warned and SweetiePie reluctantly ambled away and hopped up onto a windowsill, probably dreaming of capturing a golden retriever.

She opened her emails and emitted a little laugh, seeing she had one from Symon. He'd written, I've looked at your blog. Copy three of what you think are best on different subjects. Then we'll work on an outline. Go ahead and write a query letter.

Good grief, what was that? Oh well, he could explain it later. In the meantime, she copied one on makeup, another on exercise and the last on nutrition.

Afterward she felt rather helpless, then remembered the books she'd bought. She'd already looked them over. Okay, he'd said she should look at the index for an example of how to develop an outline.

Ah, that helped. So under makeup, she added hair and nails, and then decided makeup should go under that category and she'd call the whole thing *Grooming.* Woo-hoo, she was becoming a writer.

For the rest of the morning, while the repairmen fixed the section of porch ceiling and roof, she worked on the project. SweetiePie sat on the front windowsill watching every move as Mudd and Symon seemed to be watching the work in progress.

It was nice having someone around. A man. What would her and Wes's lives be like? Would he mow the lawn or have someone else do it? She tried to picture Wes on a mower. She laughed. Somehow it didn't fit.

Well, of course not.

Aunt B had probably had this comfortable, cared-for feeling when Symon's dad was caretaker. That's why he was called caretaker.

Looking out occasionally, she'd see Symon walking around, moving the sprinklers from one section to another and inspecting the newly planted flowers that already looked as if they'd always been there.

Symon seemed the same way. More a part of the property than she had ever been. As if he belonged here. She could understand why Aunt B had said the cottage was his home. Not because she felt sorry for him. There was no need for that. And come to think of it, the cottage rivaled, if not exceeded, the worth of the house on Jones Street.

After the repairmen left and Symon neared the back, she invited him into the kitchen and showed him what she'd done.

"Good start," he said. "Did you write the query?"

"What do I do, just say, 'Hey, you want my book?'"

He laughed. "That may need a little revising. May I?" He gestured at the coffeepot.

"Sure. Cups in the cabinet above the pot."

While he got the cup and poured the coffee, he instructed. "A couple sentences saying *Pretty Is as Pretty Does* is about grooming, exercise, nutrition…" He came to the table and pulled up a chair near her, permeating the odor of the out-of-doors. Fresh, cool.

"…and whatever other categories you will deal with. Then a paragraph going into a little more detail. You said it's for children and teens, right?"

She nodded, and he continued, "Say it is a guide for anyone wanting to—" he grinned "—enhance their appearance and health."

She gave him a sideways look and was reminded again of how pleasing he was to the eyes. She looked back at the laptop and typed.

"And the last paragraph is about your credentials. Your qualifications for writing this book."

"You mean, like the former—"

"No," he said. "Don't say former. Say you're winner of Miss Sunshine Pageant or whatever it was. First runner-up for Miss Savannah and any others. Modeling studio teacher. Describe what you do your way. Where you speak and teach. Mention your blog and all your social media."

She typed as he talked, then had that helpless feeling. "It's not as easy as you make it sound."

"I know," he said. "Like Mark Twain said, the hardest thing about writing is getting the words right. Now, do the best you can, then email it to me and I'll send it to my editor."

"May take a while," she said, looking over at him. "How long does it take you to write a book?"

"I started at age five," he said.

"Oh, so in about twenty-five years I can have this done."

"Hey," he scolded. "Twenty-four years. I'm not thirty yet. But, it's only a letter."

She looked at him askance and he looked at his coffee,

then said, "I have an idea. Mudd and I are going to Tybee this afternoon. If you'd like to go along, you can read it to me and I'll edit."

"I have a better idea," she teased. "I'll drive and you put this thing together instead of telling me how. Then I'll give you credit like you're giving credit to Aunt B for your books."

"Nice try," he said, looking a little more than amused. "Miss B challenged and encouraged. She didn't do the work for me. You do your own, and you take the credit."

"In that case, I'm not going," she said saucily, then grinned at him. "Really, I'd like to. But I have class from four to six."

"I could pick you up afterward," he offered.

"I'd like to, but..." she said, smiling over at him. He was fun. She could see why Aunt B was impressed with him. He told interesting stories, knew how to do things and seemed eager to help her. Of course, Aunt B wouldn't be thinking of him as a very appealing man. On second thought, why not? A fact's a fact. Nothing wrong with that. As long as she kept everything in perspective, which brought her thoughts back to Wesley. "Wes and I have a standing date. When we can, we meet after class and have dinner together. But if he works late, I might come out after class."

"I understand," he said. "Just work on this as you can, and we'll see what develops."

She nodded. "The firm is working on a big murder case."

"I've been catching it on the news."

"I don't," she said. "He can tell me about it later. I'm busy working on—" she emphasized "—*my book*."

Oh, this was more exciting than planting those little flowers in the dirt. She laughed delightedly, and just as quickly it changed. "What if they don't like it?"

She watched him finish his coffee, get up, and rinse out the cup and put it in the dishwasher. Apparently he'd done that before. She shrugged. "Well, it doesn't matter. That's not my life's goal. I'm not a writer. Don't plan to be. It's not as if

I'm trying to get into a writing career or anything. Besides, I'm applying for my graduate work at the college this fall."

After about ten minutes of explaining why it didn't matter she seemed to run out of breath and her face felt as if it was probably the color of those little pink anemones.

Symon stood propped back against the cabinets, staring at her with that wicked silver glint in his eyes, looking amused. He whistled. "Glad that's settled. We can just forget it now."

"Right," she said, picking up her cup, but it was a little shaky so she returned it to the saucer. "But wouldn't it be something," she said, "if they liked it?"

Chapter 15

Symon walked back to the cottage smiling, then cautioned himself about getting caught up in something that could distract him from his purpose.

However, during lunch he checked his emails and was surprised to see Annabelle's query letter already. She'd done a good job, but of course she already had a resume for her speaking engagements. And the other information was on her blog. He tweaked the information and felt it was ready to go.

Before sending it, however, he made a call to his editor, told him about her project.

"That's not my department," Jim said. "Have her send it in."

"It's only a query letter," Symon said. "Just have them take a look."

"You know this is atypical."

"So is the amount of money I'm making for your company."

Jim sighed, but acquiesced. "I'll talk to the nonfiction department. But these things take months."

"I'm not asking for publication. Just a response to an idea. If they can't use it, let me know."

"I'll give it a try, but don't expect anything for—"

"A few days. Thanks, Jim," and he rang off.

He looked her letter over again, was satisfied, typed in her Jones Street address and sent it.

He wasn't too surprised a couple hours later when Marsha, from the nonfiction department, called him. "This is a great idea," she said. "And I see this as a possibility for a wider audience than being limited to girls preparing for pageants. One thing is missing. Under nutrition she needs some recipes to make it more appealing, not just food charts and calories. We looked at her blog and there's interesting material there. For females," she emphasized. "So tell her to work up a proposal and I'll take it to committee."

"How about you telling her in a letter. Officially?"

"Sure," she said. "Thanks for this."

He felt like running up there and breaking the news. But it wasn't really news. It was still just a possibility. He felt a sense of excitement about this and quickly told himself he'd felt it before, at writers' seminars when he'd encouraged or taught an aspiring writer.

He thought about that. Yes, he knew she was Miss B's niece. Wesley's fiancée. And he needed to concentrate on what he came here for. His book about Miss B and ideas for his own future thrillers.

It was late afternoon when he arrived on Tybee. The two women were waiting on the balcony when he drove up and stopped to roll down his window.

"The door's unlocked, just come on up the steps and through the house," Miss Clovis called.

They stood, smiling like they were extremely happy when he opened the glass doors and stepped out.

"Oh, Symon," Miss B exclaimed as she opened her arms to him. He hugged Miss Clovis, too, all the while thinking Miss B's hug had been just a little warmer, a little longer, more intense than he'd known before. Or maybe that came from him. But it felt like a welcome home.

"Oh, just let me look at you," she said after Clovis moved away from him. "You look wonderful. Older. I mean more mature."

"And you two look the same. Beautiful as ever."

Miss B really was. He never evaluated her appearance. Just knew everything seemed perfect. She was a gracious, lovely lady. He'd watched her around some people and she'd seemed rather stiff. But he knew her as pleasant and even surprisingly fun.

After a few expected formalities, Clovis said she had a few things to do in the kitchen and Miss B said he and she might walk on the beach. "You said you were bringing your dog?"

"Mudd's down by the car. I'm hoping to reacquaint him with water. He's wary of the creek."

She petted Mudd, who came up to them when they reached the bottom of the steps, then the dog followed close behind them.

Symon inwardly reprimanded himself for having any misgivings about seeing her again. She made him feel as accepted as ever, maybe even more, and it seemed they'd simply picked up from where they left off. Maybe they were even closer. But, she had always been to him what he thought a mom would be.

She looked over at Mudd. "He's a beautiful dog,"

Symon remembered the day he'd gotten him. That big dog had been in a cage just barely big enough. Symon almost suffocated at the first look. Mudd's sad eyes didn't hold any hope, more like acquiescence of his fate. Symon walked on and made his purchases and could have walked out into the parking lot without going by the animals again. But he felt something he rarely felt. That something was compassion.

It wasn't that he didn't care about others, just that he didn't have any others to care about. That dog was messing with his mind. He was about to turn away when a woman started telling him about the awful ordeal the dog had gone through. A tornado had ripped apart a trailer, killed the elderly man who lived in it. The dog had been found with its nose barely sticking up out of the flooded puddle and his hind leg caught beneath some the rubble.

The woman said the dog needed him and he'd asked, "Why would I want a dog?"

She'd said, "It's something to love."

She'd turned out to be right. More than that, it was something who loved him.

It sounded like an apology when Miss B said, "Neither my parents nor Robert wanted animals on the property."

"But you have a wild cat now," he said and she laughed.

"I've heard how SweetiePie treats Mudd." She shook her head, then turned reminiscent again. "I got her mainly for Annabelle after Robert and Gina were killed."

"Animals can make a difference," he admitted.

They paused to watch Mudd walk to the edge of the water. He ran from the flow when it neared him, but pawed at it and seemed to think that made it move away from him. Then he began to chance playing along the edge.

"It's Mudd who got me to thinking about a permanent home, settling someplace." They began walking again. "He needs a home. Maybe I do, too. New York is not where I want to spend my life."

Her voice sounded as hopeful as her blue eyes, which looked over at him. "So you may be back for good?"

He tilted his head, indicating the possibility.

"I've told you the cottage is yours, anytime you wanted to return."

"Thank you. Right now it's the perfect place for my project. You know—" he looked at the warmth in her eyes, so accepting of him "—I'd still be like a lost little boy without your attention."

"Oh, Symon. Don't you know what a lonely woman I would have been without you?"

"You had your family."

"Occasionally. They had their own lives. You were always right there."

He was a little too old and too male to get emotional. "We'll have to get that into the book," he said and added quickly, "Speaking of books, you've never told me what you think about mine."

"I've kept up with you, Sy DeBerry. On the internet, in literary journals. Your success speaks loudly."

Not as much as her indirect response. He knew what the public thought. Her positive opinion was what he wanted most. "They haven't lived up to your expectations?"

"Oh, they've exceeded them in many ways."

"You're saying I have an Achilles' heel?"

He felt like a student again. Needed the lessons. His sales were great, but he wanted to improve in any way he could.

"I wouldn't say it's a fatal flaw. Just debatable. And not with the general public, I don't suppose."

"What is it?"

"I've read them over and over. I see you in them. Your beautiful mind. But when I read about some of those terribly evil characters I feel something is missing."

"They always get their due. You told me a million times that the stories must end good. Mine do."

"But is good the opposite of evil?"

"Yes."

"Is it?" Then as he tried to figure out where she was going with this, she said, "I've been bad in my times."

"Not you," he said in jesting way.

"I was bad to marry Brandley. You remember. You were ten years old. You recognized his meanness."

"He didn't like me."

She scoffed, "He didn't like me either, after a while. Money was his obsession. But did that make him evil?" Her voice lowered. "Was your dad evil? Your mom?"

"No."

He couldn't keep walking. He stopped and she did, too. They faced each other. She said, "Think of people you know. Some have done bad things. But were they evil?"

He knew without thinking. Brandley and money. He was bad but not evil. His dad and alcohol. His dad was a good man. He'd simply liked his alcohol or become so addicted that it became a disease. But he wasn't an evil man.

Symon knew an evil man. He'd interviewed a few for a better understanding of his villains. One in particular had exuded evil. He wasn't sorry for the atrocious acts he'd committed and said he dreamed of getting out and doing those things again. His laugh had been maniacal.

"You see," she said. "I've made bad choices. My parents made choices I thought were evil but in my more mature years I recognize their decision as making a choice between situations that weren't good. But it wasn't evil."

"I can't imagine you being bad," he said.

"Of course you can. You can imagine anything."

He acknowledged that with a small twitch of his head and they kept walking. Not talking.

Good was the opposite of bad.

Ask anybody and they'd say good was the opposite of evil.

Somehow it was beginning to seem incorrect.

"I'll have to think on it," he said finally.

Her smile was faint. "We should turn back now," she said.

Yes, he thought. She just gave him a quiz. He had no quick reply. But coming from her, he knew it was worth pondering.

"Otherwise," she said. "They're perfect."

They both knew he wouldn't rest until he'd dealt with that "otherwise."

Chapter 16

Annabelle saw them walking up the beach when she drove up. They looked so relaxed with each other. Maybe it was the evening sun, but Aunt B seemed to glow. And of course she'd seen Symon in the sun, in the shade, in the morning, at noon, at night, so she didn't have to think about him.

But a little later after they'd all sat at the table and had sweet tea and freshly baked cookies, he said it was getting close to high tide and asked if they would like to ride the waves.

"We did that this morning," Aunt B said and Annabelle started to laugh. But they didn't.

"Really?"

"Well, yes, honey. Is that a surprise?"

"I just didn't know you did that."

"Even I do that," Clovis said. "I live on the beach you know, and my philosophy is as long as you do it, you can do it."

"Who do you think taught me?" Symon said.

"Okay," Annabelle acquiesced. "Shall we all go?"

"You two go on. Enjoy it."

Symon looked at Annabelle. "I suppose you brought your suit?"

She clutched the front of her shirt with both hands. "What do you think I have on under here?" she said and then made a face. That was not the thing to say.

Aunt B and Clovis snickered. Symon smirked. "I don't think about things like that. I'm an inner beauty kind of man." He got up. "The boards still down in the parking garage?"

Clovis nodded.

Soon as he turned his back, Annabelle looked at the women and made a motion of zipping her lips.

"Go have fun, dear," Clovis said and Aunt B just looked out at the ocean.

Okay, she'd have fun, she decided, shucking out of her clothes, and met Symon in the parking garage. *My goodness gracious.* It wasn't that she didn't know about his broad shoulders, or expect a good-looking swimmer/landscaper would have a muscled chest and tight abs, she just wasn't accustomed to seeing one with his shirt off. She reached for a board. "Race you." Off she went with him right beside her.

"Haven't done this in a long time," she warned.

"Like riding a bicycle," he retorted.

So they went out, over waist deep and when the good wave came, he yelled, "Now," and she was a second too late, was deluged and stuck doing nothing while he rose and fell and glided into shore atop the waves.

"Okay," he said, shaking his head, returning to her. "I'll say now before it's time."

"That was deliberate," she sassed. "I just wanted to see if you could do it."

She really had enjoyed watching him. He looked like a porpoise gracefully gliding through the water. And she did get the hang of it and glided along with him.

"Oh, this is great," she said breathlessly when they were

standing in the deep water, waiting for another perfect wave. They missed one, or two, while she thanked him. "I really needed this," she said. "Sometimes I forget to have fun."

Then she wondered if they both did. They were just standing, looking at each other, and the sun was getting low, the tide stronger, and she was about to say they should go in when he yelled, "Ouch!"

"Ouch?"

He grimaced. "I think I just got stung by a jellyfish. Let's go."

They hurried ashore, and he hopped and looked at the red welts above his ankle. "If I recall," he said, "this is the time of year they drift up this way."

When they neared the balcony he called up to the women. "Have any vinegar?"

Clovis held up a bottle.

Apparently they'd seen him hopping around and examining his leg.

When they got to the balcony, Annabelle said she'd go ahead and shower. Symon said he'd sit there and absorb the vinegar. She felt better about that. She figured it might not seem proper for them to be completely undressed at the same time, even if there were two bathrooms.

After they were both decent again, Symon asked if he could take them to dinner.

"We ate while watching you two having fun out there," Aunt B said. "We eat early, then have popcorn and watch TV or read later on. There's a seaside restaurant down the way."

So Symon and Annabelle went. And sat on the deck while the evening turned gray, the wind picked up, the ocean churned and moved onto the shore. They ordered and he talked about how pleased he was to be with Aunt B again.

"And thank you," he said to Annabelle. "You're an unexpected pleasure."

She smiled. "Without your encouragement, I wouldn't have

done anything about that book. You've helped me look at some things in a different way. I'm grateful."

For an instant she thought about having associated with Symon more in a few days than she had with Wes in a month or so. She'd shared some of her deepest thoughts about her life and plans that she and Wes simply didn't have a chance to discuss. Not that there was anything wrong with it. If Wes hadn't had to work again, she'd be with him.

She bit into her hot dog with chili and savored the bite. Symon was quiet. Maybe he was tired. She felt tired. It was a good tired.

She looked over at him and he looked at her with his un-readable expression. "You're going to ruin me," she jested. "I have a pink nose. Now I'm stuffing myself with fat and calories?"

"No problem. The pink will become tan. This indulgence is an occasional occurrence. Tomorrow you'll return to your usual chosen lifestyle."

She looked around, not really seeing the people, fading into thoughts. Chosen? Her life had been chosen for her. But it had been a good one, a happy one, a sheltered one, until her parents were gone. She had chosen. Tomorrow she would return to her job, her friends, her responsibilities and Wes.

Return to Wes? It wasn't a matter of returning. She hadn't left him. He was putting in all those hours for her, for their future.

Her focus reverted to the other tables, families, young couples, talking, laughing, belonging. They all were being whipped by the wind and didn't care. Sand and salt were in the air, and in the hair. Something inside seemed unleashed today while riding the waves, being taken by the tide, letting go, not resisting its pull, its currents. She felt more alive than she had in a long time.

She remembered the more carefree days when she'd be at the beach with Wes. Times of holding hands, arms around each other, kicking the sand with bare feet, avoiding jelly-fish, picking up shells, their arms touching, then stopping to kiss, rather passionately at times. And when it became too serious, they'd run off toward the ocean, laughing, splashing…playing…

"Would you like to walk on the beach?" Symon's voice penetrated her thoughts.

She looked at the moonlight shining on the humming sea, saw the tide caressing the shore, ebbing, flowing. Yes, she would like it. So she said, "I should…" Return? "Get back."

"I understand," he said.

Heaven help her. She hoped he didn't.

Chapter 17

On Friday, Wes called, really excited. He was worn out. "It's over, Annabelle. Now it's up to the jury. Let's just have some down time tonight, okay?"

"Sounds great. Aunt B is coming back in the morning, so we'll have tonight alone. I'll fix something good for supper."

"I'll be…" He laughed because he usually said "late," but this time he said, "early."

During supper he talked about the case, how they were about as confident as they could get that the verdict would be in their favor. Then he said they'd have the weekend together, but he had to go away for a few days next week with his dad. After that, he'd have some decent hours.

That sounded good to her. After they cleaned up in the kitchen they went out onto the front porch with their Diet Cokes. The evening was growing cool after the hot, humid day. They sat in rockers.

Symon's car was gone. He'd mentioned a movie he wanted to see and if Paul didn't have to work he might go with him.

She'd thought if Wes had to work, she might go, too. After all, it looked like Symon, more so than Wes, was the closest thing to a family member to Aunt B, besides her. They were...what had he jokingly said? Cousins?

She chuckled.

"What?" Wes said.

"Just thinking. I had a great time at Tybee last evening." She began to tell him about riding the waves and that Aunt B still did that. And Symon being stung by a jellyfish and...

"You took him to Tybee with you?"

She heard the edge in his voice. "I didn't take him. He drove his car. I drove mine after class. We both went to see Aunt B." She huffed. "But what if I had gone with him? He's a friend and visitor of Aunt B's. And he's been a friend to me."

"I'll bet," he said and she could hardly believe what she was hearing.

"What's your problem, Wes?"

He exhaled heavily. "He's the caretaker."

"What does that mean? Not good enough to run around with?"

"Is that what you're doing? Running around with him? First it's Pirate's Cave. Then it's the bookstore. Now it's Tybee. What's next?"

She could not close her mouth.

He lowered his voice when he said, "He's going to get the wrong idea. I mean, he works for you. For Aunt B."

"Really? And who does Jennifer work for?"

"That's different."

"How?"

"She's a paralegal. She has to come along on some trips. It's business."

"Well, this is business, too. He and Aunt B are working on a book. He is helping me with my book."

"Right. And didn't you tell me he went out with Lizzie

and that had something to do with ideas about a book?" He glanced upward. "It's a line."

"A line? He hasn't pursued Lizzie although she wouldn't mind."

"Why not?"

She ignored that. "You know Celeste has wanted me to write this book. And he wants to honor Aunt B because she was instrumental in getting him into writing. You should see them together, Wes. They're close."

He shook his head. "Doesn't add up. Okay, so he and Aunt B were close. But who wants to read a book about it?"

Nobody, was the first thought that ran through her mind. Symon had entertaining, wonderful stories. But who cared? Just like who cared if she wrote about little girls learning correct posture, etiquette, fashion, makeup, nutrition. They were adorable just the way they were. She was reverting to her insecurities about it.

Who would care if Symon wrote a tribute to Aunt B?

"Okay, who would care?" she said defensively. "Symon and Aunt B. He said he speaks to writers' groups. They like his childhood stories. Oh, and his editor likes them."

"All right," he conceded. "But how is he making a living while doing that?"

She raised her hands. "I don't know. Wes, you're making me feel like I'm on the witness stand and I don't know what the charge is against the…the…" She waved her hand. "Whatever. The criminal? What's the crime?"

He sat silent for a long time. She felt hot on the inside but was getting cold on the outside. He tapped his fingers on the arm of the rocker. Then stopped. He took a drink of Coke. "Okay," he said calmly. "It's my attorney mind at work. But, Annabelle, you're different."

She started to deny that. But then raised her chin. "I think you're right. I'm putting closure on a time of my life. Which

I guess leads me to tell you, I'm not going to enter any more pageants."

After a long stare he spoke. "That is your life."

"It was. Now I want to return to school. Get my teacher's certificate."

"Annabelle." He stood and walked over in front of her, then backed against the banister. "We postponed our marriage, even the engagement, because of your pageants."

"Right," she said. "Do you want to postpone for a few more years?"

"No, I don't. I've just assumed you wanted to go on to bigger pageants. I'd wait for you. I have waited for you."

"It's not one-sided, Wes. I've waited for you while you finished law school. Got established in the firm. Worked on court cases." She shook her head. "I guess it's not really settled in my mind yet. It's unsettled. I think one way and feel one way. Then I talk to you and I'm back again to where I was."

He nodded. "That's what I mean. You're different."

Different? She felt different. Like she might not be as morose as she'd been since her parents died. She was getting on with her life. "I'm making decisions, Wes."

"I think you're being influenced."

"I came out here to be alone and think about decisions."

"But you're not alone."

"I'm alone in the house, Wes. He has not set one foot in the house. Not even attempted to. Well, the kitchen. But I invited him in to see the laptop. One time. Other than that, he's come no farther than sitting on the edge of the porch. Except to paint the few slats on the inside of the banister."

Wes turned with his back to her and his hands gripped the banister. When he turned to her again, he had that apologetic look on his face. "I'm sorry, Annabelle. It's just that he's a guy. And you're a beautiful woman. He's not going to take you lightly."

"He's never done or said one word—"

"He's a guy," he repeated, as if he'd made a profound remark.

"Well, so are you. And I make up my own mind about things. About…guys."

"My girl doesn't run around with other guys."

"Fine. My guy doesn't play golf with other gals, paralegals or not, and take them to dinner."

Even in the moonlight, she watched the slow burn. The red face went away and she thought it might be replaced with ice, but he finally raised his hands. "This is going nowhere." Then he grinned. "You love me?"

Oh, how many times had she said, "I love you." He'd said it, too. They'd said it casually, they'd said it seriously, they'd said it emotionally. They'd said it after an argument or disagreement.

But they'd never argued about some other man. Why had Wes suddenly turned jealous?

"Of course, I love you." There, she'd said it as confirmation, a reminder. She'd loved him a long time. They loved each other so much she'd sort of taken it for granted. But that was all right, too. Sort of like the times she'd sung, "I love you, Lord" and later realized she wasn't even aware of the words. She took the Lord for granted. She could say she loved the Lord without emotion. She could say she loved Wesley without the emotion.

Oh, she wanted the emotion. She felt it come into her eyes and she went into his arms that opened to her. She welcomed his holding her.

It wasn't easy going from defending herself, and Symon, to feeling lovey dovey. Then she lifted her face and felt his lips on hers. She felt the emotion. His emotion. Wasn't that love?

Chapter 18

Symon noticed the change in her. As if she had lost confidence in her book project being accepted.

"Even if the publisher doesn't take it," he assured her, "there are other ways. It can still be printed, a good cover can be made, and it can be used for your classes and when you speak to groups."

"Okay, I'll keep on and you can keep giving me pointers. Thanks." But her response seemed more polite than enthusiastic.

But, he had come here for the writing of *The Cherry Tree*. Annabelle was enthused about that. After she exercised on Monday and Wednesday mornings, the two of them sat at the kitchen table, one on each side of Miss B, and looked at the photo albums.

"Aunt B," Annabelle exclaimed that first morning. "I had no idea you had all these. My goodness, this is as detailed as my parents had for me."

"Well," she said, "Symon was right here. And so was the camera."

"And the newspaper clippings." Annabelle was as surprised as he. Miss B had taken a lot of pictures, but he hadn't expected this. But she had gone to many of his hometown swim meets. And his graduations. She had not been just kind. She had…cared. He should not have stayed away so long. Should have trusted his and her feelings. But he'd been only a boy. And she never said outright…

So he did. "She was like a…" He felt a little choked up. "A mom to me."

He saw her shoulders rise, but her soft hand reached over and covered his for a moment.

Annabelle looked from one to the other. She looked very pleased. Then Miss B removed her hand and turned another page.

The three of them would sit and he would remember stories and they would laugh. Miss B would remember stories he had forgotten and they'd laugh, or wince or shake their heads.

He liked the idea of this family life. And as long as he controlled his thinking, remember who belonged to whom, all would be well. Of course, he was guilty of that excuse of being only human. But he was also a sensible man who could control his actions and his thinking. All he had to do was prove it.

One of those mornings, Miss B said he might want to go to church with them. "You still go, don't you?"

"Sure. I've attended the big ones in New York, other places I've visited. I like to see the architecture. What different ones look like. The different kinds of services and preaching. I like to compare."

He looked at Annabelle. "I went when I was young. Miss B told my dad I should go and had the van pick me up on Sunday mornings. So I went. I didn't have a family to sit with in the service so I'd walk home after Sunday School. As I got older, had a few friends who went, I went occasionally. It was cool not to go all the time."

Annabelle was astounded. "Why didn't you sit with Aunt B?"

He screwed up his face. "None of the pews had my name on them."

Annabelle looked about ready to cry until she saw Miss B with her hand to her mouth and her shoulders shaking. Then she said, "Don't believe a word he says."

Then they laughed. He could have told the truth. He wasn't about to sit with a bunch of women and he'd rather fight the boys than sit with them.

He knew Miss B, and probably Annabelle, would rather hear that he was active in a church. But that had not been his lifestyle in New York. "And," he told them, "I went to Willamina's church last Sunday. Got all those warm hugs and loud singing and amens and topped it off with Southern fried chicken."

"She only works for me when I call," Miss B said. "I don't need her all the time anymore."

"She's coming to clean the cottage for me."

Miss B smiled. Pleased.

And when Annabelle wasn't there, he and Miss B sat on her porch, she in the rocker and he against the post. Thomas Wolfe was wrong. He had come home again.

The days became increasingly cloudy. Rain and storms were predicted. "That's what I've been waiting for," he told Miss B. "Then I can see what that troublesome part of the creek is doing. Dad had to rework it many times."

Then the storms came. And true to form, that troublesome place on the bank washed out. The reinforcing plants and rocks would hold only so long and have to be replaced.

He assessed the damage. He'd need to place some stones in the water and some halfway out of the creek. He ordered plant hedges and bushes to replace those washed out. He'd use smaller stones to keep the plants in place and make it look like a part of the natural setting.

On Thursday morning, he decided to forego his morning swim and begin the work on the creek. He'd worked for a couple hours to remove the boulders and rocks so he could replace them.

He'd just finished placing the large boulders in the creek, and was ready to pile smaller ones on them when he heard his name called. Looking up, he saw Annabelle hurrying toward him. About that time Mudd streaked past him followed by the monster cat, Mudd bellowing, the cat screeching. Both animals landed in the creek, paddling furiously. Mudd would drown if that cat didn't scratch him to death.

"Come," he called, reaching toward Mudd. About that time the boulder moved. He tried to grab it, but it rolled into the creek. His foot kept slipping and so did his hands and the next thing he knew he fell on his back into the creek and waved his arms trying to steady himself and find Mudd.

He finally got on his feet and looked around. Mudd was crawling up the muddy bank. Symon rather resented Annabelle standing there, in her dry denim shorts and T-shirt, her long hair blowing freely in the breeze, pointing and laughing.

Mudd climbed up the bank without his help, the now-skinny drenched cat sat near Annabelle staring at Mudd, and Symon stood in the creek sopping wet, swaying with the current. His consternation turned to helpless acceptance and he began to laugh, too.

But then, Mudd, living up to his name, slipped in the mud, straightened and started shaking like he was at a disco. Simon was yelling, "No. Don't."

Too late.

Annabelle was screaming bloody murder and trying to get away from his muddy foot, which plopped right on her shoe, and she was waving an envelope high in the air. She kept screaming and stepped right over on the slippery muddy bank, and then was coming toward him in the creek.

Symon caught her best he could, ended up on his backside in the chest-high water, still holding on to her. He was trying to hold her up above the water. One arm went around his neck and the other was still in the air. "Not the letter," she wailed while he held her, which wasn't easy to do in the fast-flowing creek.

"It's wet," she moaned. "It's from the editor."

She seemed frantic. He wasn't exactly calm himself. "Don't worry. They have copies. You can get a copy."

He managed to get up and set her on her feet, but she clung to his biceps and he steadied her at her waist.

"But this is the original. And they like it. Said put some recipes in it. They want a proposal."

"A...proposal?"

She nodded.

He nodded. "I...we...can do that."

She smiled widely as her amethyst eyes looked into his. He saw her lips tremble. She was cold. He should lead her out.

He thought, *Save Anna, save Anna.* And what came from his mouth was a whispered, "Annie."

She was clinging to him. The current seemed stronger than the ocean waves He could not move back. All he could do was...hold her.

She looked at him. He looked at her. Her hair was stringy wet, her clothes were sopping wet.

"I've never been in the creek before."

"Nothing to worry about," he lied. "Panfish just swim right on by."

He should help her out of there. He should swim out. Climb up the muddy bank and shake himself. He felt rather shaky now. And it wasn't from the fast-flowing creek.

She moved and he thought maybe she thought the same thing. Not so. She moved closer and looked up at him and suddenly mud and cold seemed more like moonlight and roses and a dreamlike existence.

She had water on her face and a speck of mud.

He said the only thing he could say in a situation like that. "You look…muddy awful."

"Thank you," she said, "you, too."

Her arm moved to his shoulder to balance. He touched her face, her lips, and she moved closer if that were possible.

As the current flowed through him, he was helpless to do anything but ride the waves, give in, go with the flow, not fight it, just experience the feeling.

He couldn't think, only taste the sweet lips, feel them move against his own, feel her body pressing close, and then as he shivered in the cold creek, he felt her warm breath and the movement of her chest as if breathing were as difficult for her as for him.

"Annie," he breathed.

Her face moved back only far enough that he could look into it, at her sweet lips, as they said, "You called me Annie."

"Yeah. You just seem like an Annie right now."

"I feel like it." She had a little catch in her soft voice. "Right now."

"Annie," he breathed again as her hand came up and touched his cheek, and her fingers were near his lips and touched them, and then her lips were touching his, and he didn't know how a person could be boiling the water while his brain was frozen, but his arms and his lips were not frozen and nothing, nothing else mattered except holding, tasting sweet Annie.

She didn't try to get away.

Sure, it was fantasy, but he lived in a fantasy world, could imagine anything, and perhaps he was imagining, dreaming this. But he ceased to think and just—

Then reality came in the form of a voice saying, "Hello. I

thought I heard screaming. But I can't figure out who needs help."

As if he were a kid in a classroom, he felt like raising his hand when he heard Miss B's voice. But even as he and Annabelle moved apart, he needed to hold on to her. He took her hand and led her down the creek where it was shallow and they could walk out.

Miss B looked down and said, "Looks like SweetiePie had a bad hair day."

Annabelle reached her and said, "I fell."

Miss B said, "That happens."

Chapter 19

She knew the trial was over and the Yarwood firm had won the case. Wes called and said, "I have some great news, Annabelle. Let's celebrate. I'll make reservations at Elizabeth on Thirty-seventh.

She already had reservations but not about where to eat. "Oh, that sounds great." It was considered by many as the best restaurant in Savannah. "Maybe they will give me some recipes for my book."

In her lost letter, the editor said she wanted Annabelle to add some recipes in her nutrition chapter. So, both she and Wes both had something to celebrate.

She told herself the whole time she was getting ready, laying out the red cocktail dress that Wes particularly liked, that she wouldn't think about it. She'd gotten carried away in the moment.

Annabelle answered the front doorbell and there stood Wesley, looking much like he had when she first met him. The tension was gone from his face. That trial had done a number on him. But he was back, her fiancé, and wearing a dark blue suit, light blue shirt and a mixed blue tie. Those colors always made his expressive eyes even bluer.

"You look wonderful," she said.

"And you, my lady, gorgeous as always." They'd learned long ago about when and how to kiss before a pageant or going out. Tonight she wore a glossy lipstick. He looked at her lips, then leaned forward as she turned her face for his kiss on her cheek. "More later," he promised. She nodded and smiled.

She didn't want to think about kissing right now. It had been a mistake. A moment of gratitude expressed because… because she'd been excited about the letter and the creek water had pushed her. Wesley simply hadn't kissed her enough. She'd been like a beggar… Oh, she had to stop that. Quit thinking about it. Quit explaining it. It was over. Now, she would enjoy an evening with her fiancé. Like they used to do before work and life got in the way. The weeds.

Yes, it was good being treated like a queen by a handsome man who loved you. And they didn't talk about the case. He said he got a bonus and he'd share with her over dinner.

He drove to Elizabeth and led her inside. And when he said, "Reservation for Powers-Lippincott," they were seated in a windowed corner of the living room at a table covered with a white tablecloth like the others. Looking at the grand fireplace, she remembered his bringing her here last Christmas. He'd given her a heart necklace with a small diamond in the center on a silver chain.

She touched the necklace. It had been a promise of more to come, and a life they'd live together.

She felt herself drifting into her thoughts and forced them away to look at him. His blue eyes held a loving expression, as if he too were thinking of the necklace and that memorable night. It had snowed on the way home. She'd felt warm later in his embrace.

Now, however, she felt a slight shiver. The air-conditioning could chill a person coming in from the humid summer heat outside.

"Lobster appeals to me tonight." He looked over at her. "What about you?"

As long as it wasn't panfish. "Sounds perfect."

Just relax and eat, she told herself.

And that's what she did when the lobster was set before them along with the garden side dishes that featured the chef's special flair, after Wesley said the blessing and she thought, *Forgive me, amen.*

He began talking about another firm that wanted him to join them as junior partner. "After the guilty verdict came down, he called and offered me the job." He lifted a hand. "I know this means leaving your dad's firm."

She shook her head. "It's not his anymore. They just kept the name."

He nodded. "The bonus I mentioned is the opportunity to join Claggett."

"Claggett?" Her fork halted halfway to her mouth and she forgot about good etiquette. "That's the most—"

"Exactly." His grin spread across his handsome face. "At Claggett, there's room for promotion. One of the partners is going to retire in a few years. They're more politically savvy. I have a chance if I want to go into politics. I can give notice at Yarwood. Doesn't it all sound just right, Annabelle?"

"Perfect," she said.

His smile waned and he leaned back at the edge in her voice. "Wes, I'm a little tired of perfect. I'm tired of being single. Of waiting forever for…what? More money? Security? Sometimes, I want to go back to the days when we just cared about—" She put a hand to her forehead. This was ridiculous.

"Love and each other?" he said.

She looked across at him. "I know all the sayings like you can't live on love, all that stuff, but—" Oh, how foolish could she be. She sounded as if she was begging for his love. They knew they loved each other. And he'd brought her here. This special occasion. "Sorry," she breathed.

"No problem," he said. "Maybe you mean something like this."

He pulled his hand from his suit coat pocket and held a small black velvet box. He opened it and let her look.

"Wes," she breathed. Just when she was about to say she was tired of all this—well, she had said it. She'd been on the verge of giving up on him. On them. But for what reason? They'd planned. They'd agreed.

She kept staring at the beautiful diamond in a white gold setting. One she'd liked when they'd looked at rings several times. He took it from the box and reached for her hand and slipped it on her finger.

Of course it fit. They'd measured.

"Will you be my wife?" he asked.

Well, of course. This was what they'd planned for over three years. Almost from the first night her daddy had brought him and his parents to dinner. They'd liked each other. They were right for each other. They fell in love. Life interfered, but they were sensible.

And now, the perfect way. It was time for this. Past time.

"My dad says he can swing a down payment on a house. I'll make enough for payments. You can use your trust fund as you wish."

Before this, he'd said no.

His was wonderful news. She had news, too. And after all the help she'd received, she couldn't just—

"What about my teaching? My book?"

"We can work that out."

He was right. There was no real reason to wait any longer. She'd been told there were always weeds that pop up.

That little book idea was just a weed. What was a book proposal compared to a marriage proposal? Not that there had to be a choice.

She and Wes needed to get on with their lives. Like they'd planned. She remembered how excited she'd been, before her parents died, about the possibility of an engagement. A wedding.

Weeds of loss and grief and growing up had popped up and invaded. She needed to get back.

There was nothing else to do, no reason for anything else. She looked into his waiting blue eyes. "Yes," she said.

Chapter 20

Since it was Friday night and Annabelle had her Saturday morning class, Wes didn't stay after he walked her to the door. "We'll need to get this in the paper," he said, holding the hand that held their commitment. "Claggett is pleased that I'll be married. I think that helped cinch the deal."

Her dad had made remarks like that concerning a man in his firm getting divorced. They preferred married and settled. "And I need to let Aunt B know."

Of course he would tell his parents. Probably already had. After their long kiss in which she reminded herself he was a good kisser, he left and she called Aunt B who told her to come over.

She showed the ring to Aunt B.

"It's beautiful. Wesley," she said slowly, "finally gave you a ring. What's wrong, hon?"

As if she didn't know. Neither had mentioned it, but Aunt B had seen her in the creek.

"About yesterday. I slipped and—"

"Everyone slips at times."

"Not you."

"Oh, yes," and the way Aunt B said those words sounded like it wasn't just popping out with a wrong word or something. "I have. Seriously. It's something you and I need to talk about. Soon. But not right now." She held Annabelle's hand and looked at the ring.

"We've waited a long time for this," Annabelle said.

"Yes, you have. You and Wesley have been very sensible. Waiting for the right time." Aunt B must have seen the quiver in her lips. "Tell me what's bothering you."

"You've been in love, right? I think I only saw your husband a few times."

"Neither you nor your parents liked him so they didn't visit often. You were young and in little pageants then anyway, so busy. But to answer your question. I was in love as a teenager. But I learned that it wasn't really love. Or it was being in love with love, or the emotions that are part of becoming a woman. And with Brandley, the man I married. I was attracted to him. I was in my early forties then. He was acceptable to my parents because of his family's social standing and background."

Annabelle relaxed into the easy chair. She liked Aunt B talking with her personally. She'd often thought Aunt B didn't have a lot of things to talk really personally about.

"Oh, we had a grand honeymoon, even if I did pay for it. But I didn't mind. At that age and having been alone so long, I didn't mind if I had to buy a husband."

Aunt B smiled wanly so Annabelle did, too. "I didn't know all that."

"Well, there was never the time to say it. But love. Yes, there are many kinds of love. Even Brandley was a form of love. We often say love for how we feel about anything from a pair of flip-flops to the Lord. Only you can decide what your heart wants and what you want from a man you want to love. And it looks like you have decided."

Annabelle nodded and looked at the ring.

Aunt B was right. It sure looked like it.

She made sure she returned to Jones Street before either Megan or Lizzie would get home from their jobs. She didn't have a cold, but she took one of those cold pills that made her drowsy. For a while she thought that wasn't going to work, but she finally drifted off and awoke with the sun's rays teasing the window as if trying to compete with the brilliance on her finger.

Hearing Megan and Lizzie in the kitchen, she got out of bed, washed the drowsy from her face, brushed her teeth, took a deep breath, and trekked into the kitchen.

"What's with you?" Lizzie said. "You never sleep in. We wondered if we should check on you since your door was closed when we got home."

"Slept like a stone," she said. "Had a big night."

They stared as she climbed up on a stool and laid her hand on the island. Megan gasped and Lizzie screamed. "Finally."

"We haven't set a date."

They each came over and hugged her. She thought she might cry.

"I need coffee." She started to rise.

Megan waved her down. "I'll get it. You still look kind of sleepy. You okay?"

"Sure." She felt her lips tremble and hoped the coffee would come soon. Megan brought it.

"You know," Lizzie said, "you've been uptight about having to wait so long before getting married, not seeing Wesley enough, being bored, uncertain. And now that you have what you wanted you're the most happily depressed-looking person I know."

"No. Of course I'm happy about this. It's just…"

"What?"

"I…have a secret."

Megan said, "Just one?" as Lizzie flipped her hands out, palms up, and said, "Doesn't everybody?"

Annabelle shook her head. "This one's what Aunt B would call a doozy."

"Oh, boy." Lizzie looked at her like she was chocolate fudge. "Spill it."

"I…kissed him."

"You—?" that was all Megan could get out.

"You gotta be kidding," Lizzie said.

Annabelle shook her head. "Not just a…kiss. I mean, this was—"

"A doozy?"

She nodded.

"Oh, honey," Megan consoled, her blue eyes filled with compassion and she spoke low as if telling a secret. "Michael's a divorced man, you know. He had a rough time for a while and did not lead a disciplined life. And sometimes—"

"Hold it." Lizzie slapped the table. "That's TMI."

Megan groaned and sat back against the chair. Lizzie said, "Okay, so you French kissed Wesley." She shrugged.

Annabelle stared at her. Then glanced at Megan and then the table. "Not…Wesley."

"Ahoooohhhh," Lizzie howled. "You mean the hunk?"

Annabelle started to stand. "I shouldn't have said anything."

"No, no. Sit."

So she did.

Lizzie said, "I would've kissed him if he'd let me."

Megan touched her hand. "You kissed him after you got engaged?"

"No. But I was…promised to Wes."

"Why did you kiss him?" Lizzie asked.

"Oh, Lizzie," Megan said, taking her hand back. "They've been doing all that book work. And Wes has been gone. She's attracted to him."

"No." Annabelle shrugged a shoulder. "That's not the reason. I mean, yes, I do find him attractive. I see attractive men all the time. But I don't kiss them."

"Did he initiate it?"

Annabelle shook her head.

"You did?"

"I couldn't help it. I was in the creek with an envelope."

"Without a paddle?" Lizzie said and began to whoop with laughter.

Megan covered her mouth, but her shoulders were shaking and she sounded like a grunting pig.

Annabelle started laughing, too. And crying.

"Don't you know?" Lizzie said between rolls of laughter. "Everybody kisses when they're in the creek with an envelope."

Annabelle tried to wipe her face. How could things be so funny and not? "It's serious."

"Is it?" Megan questioned and the laughter died down.

'No." What a horrible thought. "I mean, we're not serious. It was…a spur of the moment thing without thinking. An impulse."

"Okay," Megan said. "If it's not serious, then forget it."

"Should I tell Wes?"

"No. No," they shouted in unison.

Annabelle leaned back. Then after a sensitive laugh, she told them about the publisher sending a letter. "I was just excited and happy and grateful."

Lizzie asked, "Is he still in the creek?"

"No, silly."

"Oh, shucks. I thought if he was, I'd like to borrow that envelope."

Her dearest friends went into hysterics again.

Annabelle slipped off the stool. "I have to get ready for work."

Chapter 21

When he was growing up, he'd look at the big house and hold resentment against those who came here, lived here. He'd resolved someday he'd own a house like this. Now he could. Now he knew it hadn't been resentment, but envy.

Now that he could own a house like this, and had grown a little in maturity, what he desired was a sense of family. He hadn't been able to give Miss B anything, only take all the kindness and teaching she gave him.

Now that he had a chance for family, for acceptance, being a welcomed guest and friend of Miss B, he'd dishonored her. Annabelle was the only family she had left.

Maybe he was making too much of it. Who could blame him? he kept telling himself.

And each time the thought came, so did the answer. Only himself, Annabelle, Aunt B and Wesley Powers-Lippincott. That's who. And anybody else who knew her.

Why did she let him? Why did she kiss him back?

He could answer that, too. It seemed deep inside just about

everybody was a desire to write a book. And he'd encouraged that in her. He hadn't instigated it. But he'd monopolized her time with his writing a book about Miss B and getting her hopes up with the publisher.

He kissed girls all the time in New York. Well, a lot of the time. And more than kissing.

Sure, he knew she was a grown woman. But he also knew she had been sheltered, or at least protected from the male population. Wesley had obviously respected her. She was a Christian trying to live up to moral standards and her faith.

And here he comes along, claiming to want to honor Miss B, and what does he do but take advantage of her niece.

He wished...

No, he didn't wish it hadn't happened. He wished he wished it hadn't.

Maybe she would just chalk it up to a weak moment. Weak moment? He'd felt the current of it stronger than the pull of the creek.

Maybe it wasn't such a big deal to her. Neither had said sorry when they'd left the creek to wash off the dirt.

He couldn't wash that off. Far from dirt, it was more like an impossible dream.

He'd have to talk to her, see her reaction again. If this was an embarrassment to her he would wrap up what he'd come for as quickly as possible and hightail it back to New York. Or somewhere. Tybee had been a possibility. Probably not now.

He really didn't want to forget. He wanted to savor it. And the whole time he finished up at the creek he kept seeing it, feeling it, reliving it, over and over. And he hadn't saved Anna; instead, he'd disrespected her. Couldn't it be called a compliment?

He guessed not.

He would apologize. She might flip her graceful hand and say, "Forget it."

And that might even hurt worse.

He kept at it, until he had the creek bank fixed. On Friday afternoon he told Miss B all was well. She'd looked out over the landscape or wherever her mind wandered, and he knew enough about her to know she was wondering about more than the bank of the creek.

Was he saving Anna? Or hurting her?

He needed to get his mind on something else so when Miss B asked if he'd like to go to their church Sunday he said he planned to see Willamina. So he went there again for those good, warm, welcome hugs and managed to sing the hymns reminding him of when he was just a little boy.

Monday morning would be the big test. He'd play it cool as he could when she'd come over for the treadmill, then they'd…relate. So he got up early as usual for his swim at the fitness center.

That's when he heard it. Almost the first thing Paul said before they jumped into the pool. "Annabelle and Wes finally got engaged," he said.

"Engaged?"

"Well, he gave her the ring Friday night. That's what Lizzie said."

So Symon jumped into the pool and so did Paul and they swam for a long time before stopping for breath. Symon didn't think he'd ever gone so long without breathing.

Well…maybe once.

He was grateful for that much preparation in facing her. But she didn't come. Miss B came out as he and Mudd were walking around the flower beds, seeing the profusion of color, looking for any weed or unwanted vine.

"Coffee's made if you'd like some."

"Sure," he said.

He opened the screen when she came to the door with it then she settled in the rocker and he on the porch, leaning against the post.

The silence seemed to speak. The landscape looked perfect, a beautiful picture of a big house, a great Southern city. Finally she set her cup in the saucer on the small table. "Our girl had a big night Friday."

He set his cup on the porch, not the step. "I heard," he said. "Paul told me this morning at the fitness center."

After another silence she said, "Everything still all right down at the creek?"

"The bank is now reinforced better than ever. But it's still the weak point. You'll need to have it looked at. Tends to erode there."

She nodded. He knew she realized he was saying he wouldn't be here to keep checking on it. He'd done enough damage.

"I'm giving a small dinner party Friday night for them. Of course you're invited."

When he looked at her quickly, she continued before he could say he had another appointment. "Wesley's parents will be here."

He leaned his head back against the post and looked at the ceiling. The repairmen had done a great job. But he already knew that.

"Of course Megan and Michael are invited. And Lizzie. Clovis will come. Willamina and Doris will cook. You could ask Paul to come if you'd like. I'd planned to have a dinner or a cookout or something for you since you're considering staying here. Oh, I know you could do it yourself, for those in the writing profession."

Yes, he could. All he'd need do is set up appearances and book signings at stores and libraries, get an article in the papers with his pen name, his book titles. Be interviewed on TV. Be a local celebrity. It's always interesting to the public when a local boy without means works his way up to success. And including Miss B as the greatest influence on his life would give him an in with the old-money, good background society.

It wasn't a bad idea. It went over well in New York and on his book tours.

It would work here.

He may have to resort to that, just get on with continuing his career, because he wasn't doing too well in trying to be part of a family, in relating like a decent, mature person.

"But," Miss B was saying, "this came up so quickly and I'm Annabelle's only living relative, so I must do this."

"Quickly," he said. "I thought this had been planned for several years."

"Well, yes. But you see, Wesley aspires to going into politics and has to be careful of every decision. Annabelle pondered continuing with pageants or getting into teaching. Now, they suddenly know what they want to do. So, yes, it's planned and at the same time rather unexpected. She's been so excited about that book, and getting into teaching."

"That's not a detriment to Wesley's ambitions, is it?"

"No. But it means a change in the way of thinking. Sometimes, any change seems like some kind of threat."

"So her pursuing the book idea was likely a temporary distraction."

"Maybe. But sometimes one has to have a wake-up call to see things clearly."

Maybe he had played a part in awakening Annabelle to knowing where she belonged and not delaying getting on with her life any longer. And Wes had resented Symon. He'd seen it.

But why would Wes care about him? Wesley Powers-Lippincott had it all. The name, the position, the acceptance. He didn't know that Symon Sinclair had anything.

Mudd seemed to have an uncanny sense of being needed and moved to the top step. Symon rubbed his fingers into the hair on Mudd's head. Of course, he had to come. He was Miss B's friend and writing a book about her. So he said, "Thank you."

By the end of the week he had his head on straight. He'd been foolish to give too much thought to some insignificant act that didn't bother anybody else. Annabelle hadn't come over for her exercise. She'd probably grow fat and ugly. Mmm-hmm.

He and Miss B talked some during the week, but she was busy getting ready for the dinner. And he spent more time with his career, and wrote his own proposal...for *The Cherry Tree*.

Chapter 22

Symon didn't want to go to the front door and have some-one let him in so he walked up the back path from the cot-tage and saw Paul and Wes standing with a couple other men. He said, "Congratulations," to Wes, who thanked him and introduced his dad, the only one wearing a suit coat and tie instead of slacks and dress shirt like himself and the others. He was introduced to Michael about the time Lizzie yelled from the back door that it was time to eat.

Annabelle seemed to stand back, but of course everyone knew her. Symon didn't care to make eye contact or make any special congratulatory remark. That wasn't difficult since they were making sure everyone had been introduced. Miss B asked Mr. Powers-Lippincott to say the blessing and after-ward said seats were not assigned and they could sit wherever they liked. She spread her hand toward the ample amount of food, saying that Willamina and her daughter, Doris, had laid everything out on the sideboard.

"I'm going to step in and speak to them a minute," he said

to whomever might care to hear, and after returning he took his time filling his plate so he could choose where to sit.

Miss B sat at the head of the table. On each side of her were Mr. and Mrs. Powers-Lippincott across from each other. Wes was beside his dad and Annabelle next to him, then Lizzie.

Symon decided to go down toward the end and sit by Michael, but Paul said his name and motioned to the empty seat between him and Mrs. Powers-Lippincott, so Symon was ensconced across from Wesley.

Mr. P-Lippincott began to compliment him. "I know Cora-Beth has worried about that creek after a big rain."

Out of his peripheral vision Symon saw Lizzie nudge Annabelle with her elbow and Annabelle returned it with a withering glance.

Apparently it had been discussed. Laughed about?

Symon kept his focus on Mr. PL's face as the man added what sounded like a compliment. "I hear you're getting it taken care of." He nodded and forked a bite of food into his mouth.

"It's done," Symon said. He could have added that he did it for Miss B. A guest, or a friend, didn't have to work when they visited. But he refrained, recognizing he needed to rein in that sensitive, impulsive nature of his.

"I met your dad a few years ago. You remind me of him." At Symon's steady gaze, he had the propriety to look down at his plate and cut his steak. Had Mr. PL asked his dad how it felt to have lost so much he could never reach out to anyone else, only the bottle? Only the landscape? If he'd talked to him, it would have been about the grounds, like he was doing with Symon now. Fine, if that was what he wanted to discuss.

Symon understood the awkward millimeter-of-a-second pause. They'd be thinking he was an alcoholic. Miss B said, "He was a true landscape artist."

Like any astute society lady trying to rescue her husband,

although Symon wasn't taking offense, had no reason to, Mrs. PL turned to him and asked, "Where do you live, Symon?"

"Lower Manhattan."

"Oooh. Nice section."

He smiled. "I have a studio apartment in an older couple's house. They travel a lot and like having me to look after things. And I house-sit."

"House-sit?" she echoed.

"I get paid to do that and it's research for my stories. It's information on some of the grand mansions in Manhattan and other places. Also background for occupations."

"What kind of stories do you write?"

"Murder mystery. Thriller."

Mr. PL responded cordially, "I used to read a good bit. But most of my reading now is court cases. Um, writing's a hard way to make a living, isn't it?"

"Except for the top ten, as the saying goes."

He wasn't always in the top ten but close enough to do more than eke out a living, and his payment for speaking was wickedly abundant.

And wealthy people were more than pleased to have him stay in their houses, use them as background in his novels and even name some characters after them. The books would then sell to all their employees, friends, relatives and acquaintances.

Here, no one except Miss B knew he was well known in writers' circles.

"So you think you might stay in the area?" Mr. PL asked. Obviously someone had been talking about him.

"Considering it. I've talked to a couple universities about being writer-in-residence."

They seemed to need a moment of silence to absorb that. He didn't add that they were more than receptive to the idea, particularly his alma mater.

"You find it enjoyable?" Wes asked. "Writing about murder and mystery?"

"About solving the murder and clearing up the mystery, yes."

"I do read when flying," Mr. PL said, beginning to show a little more interest than polite conversation. "Symon…Sinclair, is it? Haven't noticed anything of yours, but I go to Patterson, Grisham, Koontz, Corbin, DeBerry."

"That's my kind of reading," Symon said.

"Are they Christian books?" Wes asked.

"Depends on your definition, I suppose. Willamina's a Christian. She cooked your steak. So does that make it a Christian steak?"

Lizzie enjoyed it most; most others laughed politely and seemed to think on it. "I mean," Wesley said, with a slight edge, "do they have Christian content?"

Symon told himself he shouldn't act like a smart aleck, make people uncomfortable, not in Miss B's home, so he relaxed. "One of my early story ideas was influenced by the Bible. The one about a gang of serial killers."

They stared, probably thinking he knew nothing of the Bible.

Miss B grinned.

"The parable Jesus told," he said, "about the evil farmers who killed everyone the owner sent their way, even his son."

Mr. PL cocked his head sideways. "Never thought of it that way." He sort of nodded like it might be true.

"Miss B taught me I always had to have good win over bad."

Miss B added, "Even before he could write he drew pictures about his stories."

"How many books have you had published?" Wesley asked.

"Five. The sixth comes out in a couple months. Another in the works."

Symon had to analyze the situation. This was a dinner to

celebrate an engagement. But they all knew each other. He was the new one. They were just being polite and trying to make him feel a part of them. Might as well show he knew a little something other than landscaping and writing a few books about killers.

"By the way, Wesley," he said, "Congratulations on winning that case. I kept up with the reports about it."

"One of the biggest cases we've had around here," Mr. PL said and looked at his son with pride. "Got Wes in with the biggest firm around, too. He worked his—" He cleared his throat, then started again. "His extra hours, nights, but it paid off."

Wes perked up. "And it got me in the position to do what I've put off much too long. The most beautiful girl in the world and I are—" he put his arm around her shoulders and pulled her toward him "—getting married."

Wesley looked into her face and she turned toward him with a smile. It seemed to Symon like one of those she'd mentioned that a contestant wears even when she doesn't feel like smiling. He was probably wrong. It was himself who didn't feel like smiling.

And then Wes looked straight across at Symon like a guy who'd beat him out in a huge swimming competition one time by that millimeter of a second. Won?

Shouldn't have done that, Wesley. It boils my blood. We weren't competing. I never had her. Well, except for those moments in the creek, but what's that compared with a few years? I don't like the way you looked at me. Want to compete? What do you call winning? Money? Awards? Recognition?

Okay, let's go.

"Incidentally," Symon said, holding Wesley's gaze. "That big twist your firm came up with that helped win the case sounded familiar."

Wes cocked his head. "To be honest, it came from a book.

The senior partner said we can get a lot of creative ideas like that." He shrugged. "He keeps me so busy I don't have time to read much." He turned to his dad. "What was the name of that book?"

Mr. PL hesitated with a studied look on his face, so Symon said, *"Lord of the Wrings."*

Wesley laughed. "I think you'd better check with Tolkien about that."

"W-R-I-N-G-S," Symon spelled. "The title was meant to attract attention, and it did. Alludes to what the villain does to his victims' necks."

Mr. PL's eyes seemed stuck, as if that resemblance he'd mentioned wasn't about Symon's dad after all. "I've read all the books, that, um—"

Symon thought, *What do I have to do? Strike a photographer's pose? Get that expression in my eyes the photographer told me to get by thinking of the most sexy girl I could think of and staring at the camera? Unbutton my shirt enough to show the alluring swimmer-barbell-bench-pressed chest I had in the photo on the back of the books?*

"Um. De...Berry?" He was shaking his head.

Mrs. PL turned and stared him in the face, her cool demeanor destroyed. "I read those, too. You are?" Her voice rose an octave. "Aren't you?"

His glance moved to Miss B. He expected to see uneasiness on her face. Instead she looked at him with a softness one would expect from a proud, loving mom.

Yes, this was who he was. He wasn't just someone who can drop a boulder in a creek. He could drop a bombshell. So he said, "That's my middle name."

"Sy DeBerry. Wow." Mr. PL leaned back with the kind of pleasure Sy had seen on the faces of many fans. "You're quite famous."

"In some literary circles."

"Oh, don't be modest. Those books are brilliant. I guess

that means the author is brilliant." He laughed at what he must have thought was a joke, so Symon did, too. What Symon thought might have been tension at the table changed to their pleasure and asking more questions and saying they'd have to get back to reading now, of course had heard of his books and his name but didn't know that's who he was and why hadn't Miss B told them. She said, "You never asked."

Lizzie said, "We have a celebrity in our midst." She poked Annabelle. "Why didn't you tell us?"

"I didn't know," she said flatly. She did not look him in the eye, but she pasted on a smile. Good. So, she thought she had played a kissing game in the creek with the caretaker's son. Didn't know she was kissing the famous Sy DeBerry who'd kissed many girls in the past and had no doubt there'd be others.

"But I'm not the one to be celebrated tonight," he said graciously, and looked at Wes and Annabelle. Wes looked a little pale. Annabelle looked flushed. Lizzie was smiling all over herself.

And so. They all knew now. The celebrity in their midst was not Wesley Powers-Lippincott and his promotion. Or Annabelle Yarwood and her engagement ring. Sy DeBerry was. And he didn't have to landscape. Didn't have to freeload off somebody's cottage. Didn't have to have a particular girl. Didn't have to write a book about his childhood to be noticed. Didn't really need anything or anybody.

He was fine. Just fine.

Then why did he feel, during all this acceptance, like such a blooming failure?

Chapter 23

The harder she tried, the worse it got. Wes asked her if she'd known all that and she said no. The men, even Wes, went out to the patio and she could hear snatches of conversation about books, and murder, and court cases, and New York, and Lizzie said, "Your face is as red as your dress. What's the matter?"

"I feel stupid. I didn't know he was famous."

"Well, you should be thrilled."

"Why?"

She shrugged. "Just makes him more interesting."

"He's not interesting."

She went over to Aunt B and Wes's mom, who were discussing the responsibilities of the bride's side of things and the groom's. "Why didn't you tell me he was Sy DeBerry?"

"I thought you knew. You know he's a writer. I assumed he told you his pen name." She tried to explain. "Many writers have pseudonyms."

Annabelle nodded but that didn't help. He should have at

least told her before he kissed her, so she could've known who she was kissing.

He must have had a lot of fun with her little book deal.

She went back to Megan and Lizzie, who decided they should check him out on the internet. That just made her fume even more. Megan pled, "It's only a name."

"No, it's not. It's a whole different life."

"Looks like a pretty good one," Lizzie said, defensively.

Annabelle sighed. "It's just that he kept it secret. I mean, I've told him everything about me."

"You did?"

"Well, a lot. We had fun together. Talked. Worked on my book. Rode the waves at Tybee."

"Kissed in the—"

Annabelle put her hand over Lizzie's mouth. "No more of that. That was the other fellow. I don't know this one."

"Okay," Lizzie said when the hand was removed. "You hate him."

She shook her head. "I'm indifferent. So let's talk about bridesmaids."

"I have to go," Megan said. "Michael and I need to spend a little time together."

"Paul and I should go to the restaurant," Lizzie said. "Paul wants to make sure the new chef is doing okay."

The men were coming in. Soon they all left except Annabelle and Wes.

"I'll see how Willamina and Doris are doing," Aunt B said.

Annabelle was even upset with Wesley. "You sure were friendly with him to have not liked him before tonight," she accused.

"He's okay. What I didn't like was his spending time with you."

"Well, it upsets me that he didn't say he was two people."

"It's only a name. And why do you care, anyway?"

She looked at him. How could she say because she'd bared

her soul to Symon Sinclair or whoever he was. She thought they were friends. They'd grown close. They'd… "I don't. I don't care at all."

Feeling her face growing hot, she heaved a sigh. "I'm going outside for some air."

She went out on the patio.

Aunt B had said Symon could make up a story about anything. Well, he made up lies. And a person could lie by omission. That's what he'd done.

She should have heeded Wes's warnings all along.

She looked down at the cottage. Symon came out and got into his car.

Going somewhere.

Well, so what?

She marched back into the house and into the kitchen, where Wesley was talking with Aunt B. Willamina gave Annabelle a wide-eyed look as if to say, *Pretty is as pretty does*.

Well, Wesley liked her pretty. He needed pretty.

Since Symon wasn't here to see her stick out her tongue at him, she simply put her arm around Wesley's waist and he side-hugged her.

Aunt B put on her indifferent teacher expression and Annabelle didn't want to see what kind of glance she and Willamina might share.

"Want to sit on the porch?"

"Sure," he said.

They went out and both sat in rockers.

She felt duped. Betrayed. But that was okay. He probably laughed about her little book. Well, that was okay too. Like she'd reminded herself before, what was a book compared to a wedding?

She looked out across the lawn at the moonlight shining on the yellow green grass looking like a fine carpet and emitting a freshly mowed aroma.

Wesley reached for her hand and held it on the rocker arm. She smiled at him as his thumb gently caressed the band of the ring on her finger.

Chapter 24

On Saturday morning, Symon walked down to the creek to confirm what he'd concluded last night. After leaving Miss B's he'd gone to River Street, listened to some music, being alone in a crowd which he didn't mind, and sat on a stone wall looking at the waving girl.

She'd waved for years, maybe trying to tell herself her lover had gone forever, or maybe hoping he would return.

Years wasted? Symon wasn't one to waste time, or to fool himself for very long. He'd been foolish enough to think the kiss in the creek had meant something. Not the first one necessarily because he knew about attraction, acting on impulse, mistakes, human nature or whatever you might call it. It was the second one he thought about. He'd been ready to back away but she'd instigated that one.

Maybe he was kidding himself. It could just be because they'd related so well at Pirate's Cave, on the porch, at the bookstore, planting flowers, organizing her book, riding the waves at Tybee, and most of all kissing him in the creek.

Now he told himself it had been good. They'd both enjoyed it. But she'd made it clear from the first she was committed to Wesley. He had no business feeling betrayed because she kissed him then went off and immediately got herself engaged. She'd said plainly she was as committed to Wesley as if she'd had a ring.

They'd both taken a side trip from their intended destination. Hers with Wesley because he'd been away on a court case. His with Miss B because she'd been away at Tybee.

So, he'd just leave that stone girl waving to a lost lover. It wasn't his style. He had a life to live. He'd decided Wesley was an all right fellow, although it didn't matter what he thought. It mattered what Annabelle thought.

Symon would simply tell her, if she seemed uncomfortable around him, that he was sorry if she thought he'd disrespected her. He hadn't intended that. He just hadn't had much practice in self-discipline.

There, that was settled, and he wouldn't stand staring at a creek like the stone girl stared out across the river waving to a lost lover. He walked back up the path and saw Miss B sitting at a table on the patio, so he and Mudd strolled up to her. She greeted him with a hand extended to touch his, and then turned her cheek for him to kiss.

"Here's coffee." She gestured at the pot and extra cup on a tray. "I thought you might show up," she added as he pulled out one of the white wicker chairs, "You made quite an impression last night."

He reached for the cup. "Yes, as Sy DeBerry."

"They accepted you as Symon Sinclair," she reprimanded him.

He acknowledged that with a nod, and poured his coffee. "Yes, but not in the same way." He'd been esteemed as an accomplished author.

"That's right." Her words sounded like an accusation. "Annabelle feels you were dishonest with her."

"Why? Because I didn't tell her I sold a lot of books and made a lot of money?"

"Yes. That's what you do and who you are."

"I don't want acceptance because of that."

She gave him a long look. "It's what you've wanted from the time you were just a little boy. You wanted to be loved and accepted, to feel like you were a part of things, not separated by a picket fence."

He looked at his cup, raised it to his mouth and drank, then set it down. She knew him. She'd been the one who'd told him what his dad wouldn't even speak about.

"I need to know," he'd said, when he was just a boy, "even if it's because she hated me."

She said, "I can show you why your mama left."

She took him down to an apple tree. Next to it was a boulder like somebody had placed it there. He looked at the date etched into the rock."

"Under there…well, not under there. She's really in heaven. But under that rock is where your little sister was buried."

He looked at the date. Four years after he was born. His mama had left when he was four. She had a suitcase. She hugged him and said not to forget she loved him she'd come back for him. But she never came back and years later, though Miss B didn't know for sure, she heard she got killed in a train wreck.

Miss B had told him all she knew. At first his parents had been happy and loved each other. But he had his drinking problems already. He'd stop for a while, then go on a binge. He came in late, drunk, and she fussed. He got mad and slapped her. She tried to brace herself by grabbing the back of a kitchen chair. It fell over and he tried to grab her and she jerked away and lost her balance. She fell. That little girl came before he could even get her out the door.

"How do you know that?"

She took a deep breath. "He called me. It was too late for

a doctor. It happened so easily, he said, so quickly. She never forgave him. She talked to me but she was never right after that. It did something to her mind and emotions. He began to drink more. He couldn't stand the guilt. She screamed her hatred for him."

Symon realized he was nodding. "Did I see that?"

"You didn't see her break down after she was cleaned up and in bed. But she was screaming her hatred for your dad and he was crying and begging."

"I don't remember it, but I think I feel it as if it's in me somewhere."

"Formative years are most important, and become a part of us, even if we can't remember them."

Symon had touched the rock. His little sister. He said, "I should hate him."

"No." Miss B took a few steps to an oak and laid her hand on it. "He hated himself enough for everybody. He never forgave himself. I was walking in the woods one day and heard a strange noise. I went farther and hid behind a tree and watched your dad hug that rock and wail and say he didn't mean it and cry for God's and your mother's forgiveness. And in between, he nursed the bottle. I was afraid he might see me and go into a rage, so I stayed still and quiet. Finally, he lay prone on the ground, crying, and I slipped away." Tears were in her eyes. "He was a beaten man."

Symon had felt the sadness. Knew it in his dad from that day on.

Miss B had touched his arm that day and said, "Don't hate him. He lost so much. But he has you."

Now, all these years later, he lifted his head but didn't look directly at her. How had she known back then about losing? She'd still had her parents and her brother. She'd married Brandley when Symon was ten. He did the math. Almost twenty years ago. She would have been in her early forties.

He'd never asked her about her personal life before that.

He couldn't. He was just a boy and she a grown woman. He a worker and she the employer and owner of the big house and the cottage in which he lived.

But she understood so much. Everything, it seemed. His gaze met hers and she looked away, smiling wanly.

"Those were good years, weren't they?" he said. "You and I."

"The best," she said without reservation and looked directly at him. "The summers were best. I didn't have to do anything but sit on the porch, talk to you, play with you, watch you. You were my…joy." Quickly she said, "What are your plans now?"

He had enough stories for *The Cherry Tree*. He had enough ideas from which to choose for other books. But he would have those even if he hadn't returned to Savannah. He had no reason to change his plans from what he intended the day he returned to this property.

"Maybe find a place on Tybee. Or a place connected with a lot of history." He glanced at the house. "Or even a big house like this."

"What would you do with such a big place?"

"Well," he mused, "if I took the position of writer-in-residence at the university, which appeals to me very much," he said and she returned his smile, "I would have graciously invite students or faculty here for meetings, as you've done in the past. Maybe get a group of aspiring writers together. Lead some seminars. Teach them how to put their own experiences into their stories. Like you did with me." Like he'd done with Annabelle.

He realized those things had been forming in his mind. What he'd like to do. Before he got sidetracked. Maybe someday he'd meet a woman he could share such dreams with. Maybe a teacher… He shook away the thoughts. He didn't need to get into any fantasies.

"And at times just enjoy being alone. Except with a few cats and dogs."

She laughed lightly, then sighed. "Have you been to Paris?"

"No, but I'd love to go." Maybe she wanted to get away for a while. Have him go with her. He'd like to get away. A continent, an ocean away. He and Miss B could see the sights. Like mom and son. Now there was a setting for a novel. He nodded. "Sounds intriguing. Shall we go?"

She hesitated. "Not I. Not right now. I had some relatives in Paris years ago. I want someone to locate them for me. See if any of them might…need me."

Her tone and expression told him this was very important to her. She looked out across the green lawn.

"Yes," he said. "If there's anything I can do for you… other than cut your grass," he said, trying to lighten the tension, "then I will."

"There is," she said. "You can find…my real son."

Chapter 25

POW!

That was like a rifle shot. Straight into his heart. Truth, and the resounding, echoing sound of the shot, were like a mother abandoning her own flesh and blood.

Or like lightning striking the cherry tree.

A door shut in his face. Reality. But he'd learned reality early.

He was not her son. She had a real son.

Then she was saying something like, "I mean, biological son. I used the wrong word. I'm uncertain about this. I—"

He didn't know what else she was saying. It didn't matter. Permutations of a word. Synonyms. He didn't need to check the thesaurus. The word could be biological, natural, birth. They all meant what she'd said. Her real son.

His face, his eyes, were paralyzed. He was glad she wasn't looking at him. If she did, she'd see his fantasies dissolve.

He must tell a lie to himself. A lie that a kind woman had… loved him…like a mom.

She was waiting for his answer, not looking at him.

Her chin lifted, like a true born and bred Southern lady of means. She'd put him in his place.

His mama had just abandoned him again.

And she knew it. She knew he knew it.

But she'd just given him another subplot to *The Cherry Tree—Where the Truth Lies*. Maybe he should forget a book called *The Cherry Tree*…unless…he wrote the truth—put a killer in it and called it *The Bloody Axe,* or *The Bloody Acts.* Yes. The outline was already in his head.

His own true story.

Move over, George Washington. If that tree hadn't already been chopped down, he'd do it himself.

This was great material for a writer's mind.

But what was it for a person's heart?

He braced himself against feelings.

A second ago, he'd said he'd do anything for Miss B.

He would have.

Now, he was numb, clinging to that second.

"Yes, ma'am, Miss B," he said in the way a caretaker's son talked to the lady of the big house. "I'll try to find…" He couldn't say "your son." He said, "Him."

He didn't care about details, and after she gave him all the information she had, he made reservations and left on the first possible flight.

He felt like a toy. Broken.

On the plane, while thinking, he closed the curtain over the window. The sun made his eyes sting, threaten to water.

Chapter 26

"Don't you like your ring?" Lizzie asked and Annabelle realized she was twisting it.

"Well, sure. It's beautiful."

"And you're happy." Her glance lifted to the ceiling.

"Of course I'm happy. Just…bothered."

"I've never seen such an unhappy bride in my life," Lizzie said. "I'll be glad to take either one off your hands if they'd have me. Wesley or Syyyyy." She sighed.

Megan laughed, and stopped abruptly when Annabelle didn't and laid the bridal magazine on the coffee table. "You're not in the wedding planning mood, are you?"

She slumped. "I've made a mess of everything."

"Yeah," Lizzie said with mock sympathy. "You have a ring on your finger from a great guy who loves you. You were kissed by a famous author."

"I didn't know he was that."

"That doesn't erase the kiss."

No, that was true. She could relive it, feel it, even though she tried to forget it. It was weird. She'd kissed boys before Wesley. She was supposed to kiss boys back then. She was a woman now and not supposed to kiss men while committed to Wes.

"And—" Lizzie was poking the envelope "—you got a copy of that letter you told us about."

Yes, and the letter was an exact copy. With a note handwritten on another sheet of paper saying this was the requested copy. They were looking forward to a proposal. So, that made two proposals within a few days of each other.

"I just have to try and make it right. We had a great time together until I fell into the creek."

Lizzie shrugged. "That sounds like the best part to me."

Annabelle didn't feel like joking about it or making it sound trivial. "Like you, Megan," she tried to explain. "You and Michael decided not to go forward with wedding plans until he shakes that tiredness and headaches since he had the flu." She lifted her hands. "I can't go forward until I try to get back to a comfortable feeling with Symon. I don't know what he must think of me."

Their expressions seemed to be sympathetic. The sooner she took care of this, the better.

Upon arriving at Aunt B's, she didn't see his car. Good. Maybe she wouldn't have to chance his showing up.

"Come on into the kitchen," Aunt B said, as if consoling, apparently seeing misery on her face. "Let's have some coffee and talk."

Over the steaming cup, Annabelle said, "You saw us…."

Aunt B's eyebrows lifted. "Do you want me to have seen you?"

Annabelle sighed. "I know you did. You both must think I'm…awful."

"Frankly," Aunt B said seriously, "it didn't look awful."

Annabelle tried to smile. "Well, no. That wasn't awful. Just my doing that. It's like I've been in a different world lately.

Like I had forgotten how to have fun or something. I don't know how to explain it."

Aunt B said, "Like those little buds on the plants that just open up and blossom?"

Annabelle looked at her cup and lifted it for a sip. She couldn't think of a better analogy. As she set the cup down, she realized something. "Aunt B, you too. It's like you have blossomed around him."

"I love him," Aunt B said with feeling. "Like a son."

"His feelings for you are mutual," Annabelle said without hesitation. But she needed to get back to her own behavior. She didn't…couldn't feel about him like a mother and son. She almost laughed at that.

She tried to explain. "He's fun. And it's just that I'd been so tired of waiting for Wesley." That was no excuse for the kiss. Helplessly, she gazed at her aunt. "I love Wesley. You know that."

Aunt B was nodding. "Yes, I do. Because of love, Symon has gone to Paris for me."

"Paris?" she squeaked.

"Yes," she said. "To do what I've wanted done for forty-five years."

"Why now?"

"It couldn't be spoken of as long as my parents were alive. It was done. Over. Never to be spoken about. Your dad never knew. I couldn't bring that up to him and your mom. But in the past year or so when I've been thinking of retirement, your getting married, all the people I've lost. And this is something I have to know."

Aunt B looked uncomfortable and fidgeted with the handle of her cup. Then she looked over at her. "It's time I told you about it." She got that faraway look of hers and began an incredible story.

"I had a glorious love affair when I was sixteen," she began reminiscently. "To love and be loved and just be near the person who is your heart is wonderful, exciting, delightful and you tend to forget anything, or allow yourself to forget anything but the person and the moment."

Annabelle loved the idea of Aunt B having been so in love. But then her aunt's expression changed and her gaze lowered to the table. "I became pregnant," she said. "Only then did my lover tell me how irresponsible I was to have allowed that to happen."

Aunt B lifted her hands. "I was young and naive. But still, I cannot claim I didn't know right from wrong. I simply did not want to think of this great love of ours as wrong. Frankly, I didn't think at all."

A great sadness seemed to sweep over Aunt B. "He had a fiancée in Boston. I was just his Paris fling. Anyway," she said, "my parents forced me to give up the child. Otherwise I would be a disgrace to the family, to their friends, and a possible hindrance to my father's political ambitions. He was running for senator at the time."

Annabelle was astounded. She'd had no idea her aunt had this in her life.

"While they were campaigning for senator, I was spending the summer in Paris. He was elected. There were photos taken of me, and the private school where I would enter into my senior year. But there was no scandal. After he was elected, there was no interest in me. I was just his teenage daughter who would be studying French in France, if anyone cared to inquire."

Annabelle got up to get a tissue for Aunt B and one for herself. Aunt B wiped her eyes and smiled wanly. "It was never mentioned again by my parents. And your dad never knew. But as long as they were alive, I had to keep it to myself. Only through my prayers and the presence of God could I deal with it. Now, I need to know about my little Toby. Oh," she said, making a sound like a snort, "he'd be in his mid-forties now. For forty-five years I've wanted to know how he is."

Her eyes brightened. "I might even have grandchildren over there in Paris."

"Does he know about you?"

Aunt B shook her head. "Oh, he might know he was adopted. But he wouldn't know about me. That was settled forty-five years ago." She paused. "Symon will know how to find out information without revealing the reason. I just want to know if…anybody…needs anything."

Annabelle could stay seated no longer. She rushed over to Aunt B. They hugged and cried. "I don't even cry about it much," she said. "It hurts too much, even now."

Finally, a question nagged. "Did Symon know?"

"No. But he does now. But I couldn't have anyone else do this, then come here and drop in information that would hurt Symon worse."

The way Aunt B looked at her melted her heart. It was in her aunt's eyes. The love. And Annabelle remembered the pictures. The adorable little boy in so many pictures. He'd been Aunt B's protégé. Her…substitute.

Oh, my. How must Symon feel?

Aunt B detected that, as if she read her thoughts. She'd likely thought it herself.

"I've taught him the difference between lies and truth. It's time I let him know this truth. The secret I've kept from us all. I had to prove I could be a good mother. I proved it to him. But I loved that boy as if he were my own. I know, right now, he thinks I just used him."

"What will it do to him?"

"It all depends upon what he does with the information. Only he can answer that. But no one should ever look upon another person as the central figure in their lives. This will do to him what any trial or crisis does to a person. It either breaks, or makes a person. But I had to do it. He has to learn he can't depend on success, nor on me. Only on the Lord. Even if he hates me, this is a crisis time for him."

Annabelle's heart went out to Aunt B and Symon. It seemed her own concerns were minor in comparison with the magnitude of what they faced.

Symon must feel like saccharin, instead of the real thing.

Chapter 27

Since Aunt B would be keeping an eye on Mudd, Annabelle offered to help. He didn't need to be let out during the night, but Annabelle could tell he was lonely. After her treadmill exercise she walked with him along the creek and she decided to see what SweetiePie might do. Their creek experience seemed to have helped their relationship rather than hinder it, contrary to her own.

Aunt B let SweetiePie stay close and Annabelle held Mudd. Then SweetiePie jumped up on top of the fence. Mudd barked. They both got on their stomachs and eyed each other from opposite sides of the fence.

Apparently SweetiePie wasn't going to attack and Mudd was standing his ground. Annabelle knew he missed Symon. He'd walk around through the cottage looking for him. She began to spend a little time in the cottage herself, with her laptop, working on the *Pretty* book, typing in recipes as the editor had asked. It had more meaning now, not just something for her, but a mission that Symon had taken time with.

She thought of the cottage in a different way. It was a cozy, comfortable, nice place. She liked it. She couldn't imagine her and Wes living there. He wanted something more contemporary.

Often she sat in a comfortable recliner, aware that Symon might have sat there, with Mudd at her feet.

She could imagine…but mustn't.

That…wasn't her talent.

Wes wasn't too keen on her time with the dog, as if Mudd were competition or something. Nor did he like it when she cancelled her date with him when Aunt B called on Saturday saying Symon was returning from Paris. Not even a week had gone by since he'd left.

The three of them settled at the kitchen table. Aunt B seemed anxious, fearful. Annabelle was concerned. A tired-looking Symon focused on the manila envelope he laid on the table with his hand on top of it.

They waited. Finally he spoke. "Your cousin still lived in the same house. She took me to see Dr. Henri Beauvais. He's the adoptive father."

"Did you see…talk to Toby?"

Annabelle saw the stiffness on Symon's face. He shook his head. "Only Dr. Beauvais."

"Wh-where were…?" Aunt B breathed out. Annabelle thought her aunt did not breathe in.

"The second Mrs. Beauvais died four years ago."

"Second?"

"The first, Rosa, Toby's adoptive mother, died in her early thirties. Cancer. She'd had cancer when she was a teenager. Could not have children."

Aunt B's voice was a whisper. "And you…couldn't locate…Toby?"

Symon closed his eyes for a moment. His tongue licked his dry lips. He stared at her and Annabelle knew they both had read his mind.

Aunt B said bravely, "You don't have a good ending for this one?"

"He was not well. He was only eleven when—"

The edges of her nose flared only slightly with the rise of her chest. "He's…with God."

"Yes, ma'am."

"I suppose," she said after a long moment. "This will be closure. But I never got to tell him—"

"Dr. Beauvais told him."

"Oh? But he didn't know—"

"He knew you didn't want to give him up. That you loved him. That was…enough."

She looked at the envelope. "He sent pictures?"

"No. He said those had been put away after his first wife died and he married again. He will get them out, sort them, write to you about Toby and send pictures."

"Then the envelope is proof—"

Symon interrupted. "That he's with God. Included is a copy of Toby's baptism certificate."

"Thank you," she said.

He pushed back from the table.

Aunt B looked up at him. "Give me a while," she said. "Then we must talk."

"Mudd and I will be leaving soon."

"Symon," she said and although his back was turned to her he stopped and stood like a stone statue. "You were like a son to me."

He looked over his shoulder. Like quiet thunder he said with clouds in his face, "I'm glad I could be a substitute son."

"Yes, and was I not your substitute mother?"

He turned then and bent to lay the palms of his hands on the table. "When I asked you to adopt me you said no."

Her words were like arrows, matching the look in his eyes. "Don't you know why? If I had adopted you I would have given you everything I had. You would have become like the society people you didn't like. You would have had everything without working for it. It would have satisfied my heart, but it would have ruined you."

"You told me that my daddy needed me."

"He did. And you needed him. You needed to experience the difference in people, in life. You needed that challenge."

They stared at each other. "Like I said, you were a son to me. You are. Whether you stay or go, the cottage is yours. I don't mean to live in. I mean it's willed to you. Now, we must talk."

He straightened. "Or?"

"Or..." Her chin lifted. "Or...I'll never speak to you again."

"If we don't talk then you'll—"

She grinned, weakly.

He blinked.

So did she.

He shook his head and breathed a reply. "Yes, ma'am. We'll talk."

"Tomorrow," she said.

Annabelle thought they both looked as if they needed someone to hug them, hold them, comfort them.

And it seemed to her like an afterthought when he looked at her with tired eyes and said, "Good night, Annabelle."

She felt like it was goodbye.

Chapter 28

The congregation was singing when he walked into the church. He'd slept like Mudd for the past two nights, like an unmoving log, probably from the stress and long flight from Paris, and the long talk he and Miss B had had far into the evening.

He'd offered to take her out for dinner the night before, but she'd preferred they sit in rockers on the front porch. Later she fixed a light supper for them. Then they had coffee in the library where he'd spent so many hours in his younger days.

He accused her of not caring about him for his own sake. She'd only taught him, talked to him because she couldn't have her real son. He was cardboard to her. "Just a substitute."

"So was I," she rebutted. "For your real mom."

"I don't like the word *substitute,*" he said.

"You, the wordsmith, don't like a word that is one of the most precious in all of language, all of history?"

He knew where she was going before she said it.

"Jesus," she said, "was the greatest substitute the world could ever know. He took our place on that cross."

On a much smaller scale, Symon had taken Toby's place. Miss B had taken his mom's place. Maybe it wasn't such a bad word after all.

"I know you feel used, and hurt. As if I wanted you to be Toby. And I did envision that when you became an adult, you'd find him for me. Not for him to replace you. But you two could be like brothers. I had to let you know about him because you both are my family. And I had to know if he or any descendants needed anything."

They talked freely, clearly, and he admitted, "I couldn't have made it without you."

She shook her head. "I thought I couldn't make it in those young years after I had to give up Toby. I felt like my parents abandoned me, like you felt your mom abandoned you. My parents put political career ahead of me and their own grandchild. That's what hurt so much."

"How did you get past that?"

"Only with the Lord's help. He brought you to me the first time. Now he has brought you to me again. For the purpose you just fulfilled for me. You and I are bonded, by choice. You may leave me. I may leave you. But if you choose Jesus, he never will."

He felt like he was in Sunday school again. "I'm not a child anymore."

"Oh, yes. We're all God's children. Little needy kids, no matter how old we get."

There was no need to run off to New York. He would begin looking for a place. His initial reasons for returning were still the same, honoring Miss B with *The Cherry Tree* and that yearning for family.

Having made that decision, he decided to go where his friends went Sunday morning. When the song ended and they bowed for prayer, he took a seat on the back row and his eyes scanned the sanctuary. Paul must have been looking for him. He looked back at him and motioned with his head, indicating he'd saved him a place.

Symon didn't want to walk all the way down the aisle and in front of others to sit by Paul on the pew. Lizzie was beside Paul. Megan and Michael were there. In the row in front of them were Aunt B, Annabelle and Wesley.

No picket fence separated any of them. And yet…he felt separate.

They were friends…and family.

Lizzie leaned forward and said something to Annabelle, who slowly began to turn. He looked straight ahead. With time, he'd forget that for a moment she'd seemed to be his.

And then a man walked out of the choir and stood behind the podium. He began singing about being able to stand only when he was on his knees. The air seemed to throb with the words, "I can't even walk, without You holding my hand."

Then the preacher chose the worst verse he could for his sermon. "Jesus is the truth.…"

Symon had had enough of that lately. He'd come here with a lot of "what-if's" and now he'd discovered more truths than he'd been prepared for.

Truth? He was a hindrance to Annabelle. He saw it on her face the night of the dinner. She'd been distant the night he returned from Paris. She wasn't comfortable with him anymore. He'd spoiled that.

Truth? He couldn't be a friend to Annabelle. He couldn't see her and pretend he hadn't touched her, hadn't wanted her for his own.

His explanations to himself hadn't erased it any more than they had erased what moved into his heart. No, he couldn't pretend that. He couldn't sit there and listen to a sermon and pretend to be something he wasn't. There were many places he didn't belong and this was one of them.

He should go.

He got up and hurried out of the church and returned to the cottage. He went to the creek. Remembered his dad, who'd done his best. And a lot of what he'd done had been very good.

He touched the rock where his little sister was buried. He thought of his mom, who had abandoned him. Now, he thought her abandonment had been much like his dad's. It wasn't him she had abandoned, but her own inability to accept some things in life or to change them.

He thought of Annabelle's laughter. It had echoed through the trees. It bubbled out like the creek caressing the rocks in the stream. The leaves clapped their hands.

Now they just shivered, trembled or drooped, still like moss hung after a rain, dripping like teardrops falling from the trees. The leaves didn't clap in glee; the Spanish moss let their tear drops fall.

His own teardrops stuck in his eyes, burning and stinging his cheeks.

He looked at the creek. He would take all his memories and put them into character. Kill them. Even Annabelle in the creek. And so, looking at the creek where he and Annabelle had stood, muddy, wet, cold, he felt the warmth of the girl he wanted. The one he wanted in his arms, in his life, and he didn't know if he'd ever get her out of his heart. He couldn't have her.

And he looked at the creek where he and his dad had worked together. They'd been family. And he remembered scattering his dad's ashes and watching them float away down the creek.

He thought of how Miss B had managed. Without her son. Without her parents. Her brother. Her husband. Him, for a while.

And him? Without his mom. His dad. Miss B recently when he believed she had abandoned him, not loved him. Annabelle.

Was being Sy DeBerry the answer?

He turned. The toe of his shoe caught on a rock and he stumbled. Only slightly. Just enough to make the air throb with, "I can't even walk without You holding my hand."

Then it came.

And he looked at the Miss B's creek and knew it wasn't hers at all; it belonged to God. And it was his burning bush.

He was not a stupid man. Well, maybe about himself and others at times. But not so stupid as to turn away from a burning bush. And so, he walked over to the bench beneath the trees and he dropped to his knees and propped his forehead on his closed fists and shut his eyes tight and heard only *I Am*.

He lifted his hand. And felt as if he was being pulled to his feet standing, while still on his knees. The world was blurry. He was looking through a glass darkly. He was like Spanish moss. Swaying, adrift.

But he was attaching to the mighty oak.

Good was winning over bad.

And as if the sun broke through a storm cloud, he knew the word Miss B had wanted.

He didn't just know it.

He experienced it.

Chapter 29

After church, Annabelle stood with the others, talking about what they might do for lunch. Michael suggested the cafeteria. He liked to pick and choose. Paul looked back. "Symon was here, but I don't see him now. I'll go see if he's in the parking lot." He hurried away.

"Unless he's out there and goes with us," Aunt B said, "I'll just go on home. I think he might be thinking of leaving."

"Leaving Savannah?" Annabelle said.

"At least the cottage. He's still uncertain. But he's done what he came here for."

"Surely he wouldn't just go. I mean, without saying good-bye." And she remembered Friday night, thinking that was the meaning of his good-night. "I mean, to all of us."

"Well, he still could. He wouldn't just drive off. I meant soon."

"Tell him I need to talk to him before he goes."

Aunt B nodded and slipped out of the pew.

Wes said, "I think I'll pass on the cafeteria idea."

Megan looked at Michael and he said, "Okay, see you later," and they left.

Lizzie grabbed her purse. "I'd better find Paul or I'll be walking home."

Wes moved to the aisle and Annabelle followed. "Where we going?"

"Where you wanted to go," he said.

He opened the passenger door for her, closed it, got inside and started the car while Paul and Lizzie stood looking at them. Wes looked stoic, so she asked, "Are we headed for another argument?"

"No," he said without looking at her, while driving out into after-church traffic. Her thinking that he might dump her off on Jones Street changed when he headed toward Aunt B's.

"We going to eat with Aunt B?"

He gave her a sidelong glance as if she'd said something stupid. She knew she had.

He pulled onto the property and up the long drive. Symon's car was there by the cottage. Wes pulled up farther, near the walkway, and switched off the engine. They got out and walked to the steps, where he stopped.

She turned toward him.

He gave her a long look. "I'm not going to argue with you anymore, Annabelle. I've acted like a jerk because I've seen the difference in you. It started when I first saw you on the porch with him, relating, laughing, looking less uptight than you have in a long time. I've seen it more than once. That spark in your eyes when you talk about him."

She opened her mouth to defend herself but didn't when he shook his head. "You were more excited about hearing from an editor than you were about getting a ring from me. I feel like the diamond is a rock on your finger. A heavy one. I know it's not your fault. It's mine. It's life."

Her head was shaking. "He doesn't even talk to me anymore."

"I can't read his mind, but I know a lot about you. And I know this—you're every man's dream."

She had been Wes's dream. They both had dreams. Plans. But she wanted to be someone's reality.

Blinking away tears, she saw the sadness in his eyes, on his face. She wanted to comfort him like he'd done for her after her parents died. He'd been a safety net. He'd been there when grief returned and threatened to overwhelm her. He and Aunt B and her friends.

"I don't think you need me anymore, Annabelle. Do you?" He waited.

She could only stare.

"I love you. I've waited until you would be ready. You still aren't. You've had excuses. I've tried to be what I thought you'd want." He shook his head.

"Oh, Wesley. I do love you. You're the most generous, kind, sweet person—"

He held up a hand. "You're right."

They both made sounds akin to uncomfortable laughter.

"I have a lot of reasons you should love me. But do you love me without a reason? Do you want to marry me?"

Her breath came labored. Her right hand was trembling against her left one.

"Annabelle, I've wanted to see that special spark again. Maybe it was there a long time ago. And then there was the death of your parents. College to get through. Your ambitions. Mine. Your friends' problems. Aunt B's needs. There's always something."

She wanted to be held, and she leaned forward. His arms took hold of her shoulders. She lifted her face. His lips found her forehead. She felt them, warm, sweet, kind. And then he moved away.

She could only stare at him.

Until…she took off the ring.

He took it. Her future, her life, her hopes and dreams

turned and walked to his car, and she couldn't even lift her hand until he waved first.

He drove away.

He was gone.

Wes was gone.

She hurried into the house.

Aunt B was in the kitchen.

"He's gone."

"Who?"

"Wesley."

"Oh."

She knew Aunt B felt like she felt. Some things, some people, when they're gone, they're gone forever. Wes was still in the world, but he was gone. Who else was gone forever?

"I'm not engaged anymore. I did love him."

"I know," she consoled, with a comforting hand on Annabelle's arm. "And you would have had a good marriage...if."

"If the weeds hadn't grown in my emotional garden. I never was good at telling weeds from flowers. I've really messed everything up."

Annabelle stepped back and stared at Aunt B, who asked, "Are you all right, hon?"

She shook her head and let the tears fall. "I feel bad because I don't feel worse."

Aunt B's face was sympathetic. "How was Wes? Angry? Hurt?"

She contemplated that. "No. He knew it was coming before I did. He seemed the same, but he saw a change in me. I think he's just...sorry." She had to sniff and wipe her eyes again. "I am. Both sorry and...what's the word?"

"You're sure it's over for good?"

"Yes." She grimaced and looked down at the tissue in her hand, adding quietly, "Regardless."

"Then the word you're searching for might be...*relieved?*"

Annabelle nodded. "I think he feels that way, too. He's

ambitious and our goals are going in different directions. He'll be okay."

Aunt B smiled and nodded, confirming that. "Yes, he will. He's a fine man." She paused. "Remember what I told you when you asked how I was doing after learning that Toby died?"

"You said when some things are final, it's healthy to grieve, but think on positive things and concentrate on good memories if the situation calls for that."

"Now," she said. "I was getting ready to fix some lunch. Why don't you call Symon and see if he'd like to eat with us?"

Annabelle scrunched up her face and shook her head.

Aunt B smiled. "You said you wanted to talk with him."

"He will leave, won't he? I mean, he has to."

Aunt B motioned to the window. Annabelle looked and saw Mudd and SweetiePie lying together on the patio as if all was well. "Maybe he'll at least let us keep the dog. Oh," she said, "there he is now."

"I'll go patch up my face." She headed for the bathroom.

Chapter 30

Symon changed into jeans and knit shirt, aware he'd have to take the suit pants to the cleaners for the dirt stains on the knees. Maybe the Lord would be able to clean up after the mistakes he'd made. At least he was forgiven. He could ask that of Aunt B and Annabelle.

Walking out back to the path he didn't see a car in the driveway, which probably meant no one else would be at the big house. He'd check to see if Miss B was there.

She arrived at the back door before he knocked.

"Come on in, Symon," she welcomed him.

He followed her into the kitchen, but didn't sit although she did. He held on to the back of a chair opposite her.

"I know the word," he said.

A small gleam appeared in her eyes, but she waited for him to say it. "You're right. The opposite of evil is not good. The kind of evil I deal with in my books needs that balance."

She waited.

"The opposite of evil is holy."

She sat still. "Evil comes from Satan so holy can only come from God."

Aunt B's cheeks plumped with her smile. "I think you were taught that a long time ago. The most awesome thing in the world is being a child of God."

"I have known it," he admitted, "but it hasn't been an active force in my life. I want it to be. I couldn't see this before, but now I can see how my books will be so much better with that trait in them."

"How do you intend to do that?"

A rush of gratitude for her swept over him. She taught best by asking questions, making him think. "I don't know," he said honestly. "Since forgiveness has been on my mind a lot lately, maybe something like the ending being more than court justice wins. Characters might forgive the villain who takes from them." He shrugged. "I'll work it out. Right now, I have to work on this." He patted his chest and then pointed to his head.

"You're not alone in that, Symon. We never stop learning."

That didn't matter. "I've acted immaturely. Was about to again. Run back to New York or—" he lifted his hand, indicating nowhere in particular "—but I like my original idea of finding a place around here. I want to relate to you. It doesn't have to have a label. I love you for who you are and what you've been to me. I cherish our relationship."

"Oh, Symon."

She was getting up. If she wasn't careful she'd make a grown man blubber. She held out her arms and he was already there to embrace her. "Apart from my other son, or your mother, you and I are like mother and son to each other. There's no denying it. That will always be."

That did it.

He reached for the tissue…and someone…handed it to him.

Annabelle?

Okay, first he was scum in the creek and now he was a baby.

"I—I need to—"

"I—I want to—"

They both began to talk at the same time and stopped. Miss B said, "Why don't I whip up some lunch while you two go out back and talk. Any requests?"

Annabelle said no and hurried out the back door. Symon leaned toward Miss B. "Depends on how much crow I'm going to eat first."

"Oh, just wash it down with a little creek water," she said and winked.

He could appreciate the humor, but the timing was definitely off. Reminded him of Lizzie having poked Annabelle at the dinner. Maybe they'd all laughed about it. But Miss B had seen it.

He grimaced and went outside to join Annabelle at the white table.

"I want to apologize," she said, beating him to the punch.

He motioned for her to continue.

"I've been very angry with you."

He could take that. Even though it seemed she'd been in on the kissing as much as he, he'd already lectured himself about his part in it. He was responsible for his own actions, regardless. He nodded.

"Maybe it's kind of like you felt when Aunt B told you she had a son. You felt she'd used you, or not been truthful, or hadn't been honest with you."

He didn't quite make the connection and then she said, "I enjoyed every minute relating to you as Symon Sinclair. I respected you as a landscaper and a struggling writer. You didn't tell me the whole truth."

"It didn't seem the thing to come out with at first. Then there didn't seem to be the appropriate time. And I wanted you to accept me just as Symon Sinclair."

"I did. It's just harder to relate to a famous New York writer."

That's what was bothering her? Those sad amethyst eyes were getting to him. "I could give it up."

Her mouth opened and she gaped. Finally she said, "You'd give up writing…for…me?"

"No," he scoffed. "I'd give up New York. Writing is my life."

Her lips twitched. He couldn't tell if she was about to smile or frown or what. But there seemed no way they could get back to the easy camaraderie they'd had from the time they met. "But look," he said, "I shared almost everything with you." He heard what began to be desperation in his voice. "So, I kept it secret that I sold a lot of books and made a lot of money. Can you forgive me?"

When she didn't respond right away but seemed to be twisting her hands on her lap, he exhaled a deep breath. "If I could, I'd spend a lifetime making it up to you."

"I have one," she said.

"One what?"

"Lifetime."

While he was still pondering that, she said, "Why did you kiss me in the creek?"

Now they were getting to the real problem. Something they had to face before they could let it go. How honest could he be? Even with himself? But he began with all the things he'd told himself. The explanations. Reasons.

"Hold it," she said. "What was the name of that letter you had me write for the editor?"

"Query?"

"Yeah. Query. Okay, you're going into a long spiel here. Narrow it down to one sentence."

He'd decided to take all the blame if necessary, apologize, ask forgiveness, get out of her way and get on with his life. But now he sat confused, looking into those blue eyes, watching words form on those red lips that he'd tasted, and seeing how the breeze lifted her long hair and brushed against the sides of her beautiful face.

What was she doing? Did she want to hear that she was the most beautiful, wonderful girl in the world? But it wasn't just her looks. It was just her. She seemed to be deliberately making him suffer.

All right, Lord. If I hadn't committed myself to you a little while ago maybe I could make up something. Maybe you could give me a little...holiness? Truth.

He'd tell her the truth. That might mean she would no longer be comfortable with him relating with her and her friends. He started to say, "Many reasons," but to narrow it down to truth, he said, "Because you're the kind of girl I could fall in love with."

Her shoulders rose and she seemed to be twisting her hands on her lap beneath the table. But she asked. He had to tell her.

"So it could happen with any girl like me—?"

"There are no other girls like you."

She just kept looking at him, but he didn't know how to make it right. How could he regret it? "I can't erase it. It happened. And I am sorry if it's spoiled anything between you and Wesley. I won't try to interfere. Or relate in any way that makes you uncomfortable." He had to ask. "Was it so terrible?"

She looked directly at him. "It messed up my whole planned life."

"It was a mistake. Let's just move on."

"If you keep talking like that I might have to beg Wesley to give the ring back to me." She brought her hands up to the table and rubbed her bare finger. Did she tell Wes about the kiss? He broke up with her over it?

He gaped at it, at her, and she kept looking at it. He wasn't sure if her lips were turned in a grin or grimace. "I tried so hard to relate to you just as Aunt B's guest. I told myself you were just a man who cared about her and worked on the property. And I tried to accept you as a friend. But I couldn't. I can't because…"

Shaking his head, he pushed back from the table and stood. He mustn't imagine—

"I have a secret," she said.

He turned away. "Not good enough." He started walking.

"Sy…muuun."

He picked up his pace.

"I couldn't because I love you."

He slowed and looked over his shoulder.

She got out of her chair and he turned toward her. She ran all right in those high heels. They met in each other's arms and they both were saying, "I love you."

And they sealed it with a kiss.

When he came up for air he said, "You had me worried. It was either that, or I'd have to go jump in the creek and never come up." He looked over at the cherry tree. "I could not have imagined this. That someone like you could love me."

She tilted her head toward Mudd and SweetiePie lying together, peeking at them. "If they can do it, we can try."

"Okay, then," he said, finding breathing to be difficult. "I have a proposal to make."

"Oh, my." The tilt of her face to his was tempting him and her amethyst eyes were teasing. "Another one of those proposals?"

"This one is for that lifetime you mentioned. I love you. I want to spend my life with you. I want—"

The back screen door opened. Miss B waved at them. "Lunch," she said, and went back in.

Annabelle said, "Yes. Yes. Yes. You may be a son to her, but you're going to be my caretaker."

"My privilege, sweet Annie," he said, and sealed the commitment with a kiss.

* * * * *

REQUEST YOUR FREE BOOKS!

2 FREE CHRISTIAN NOVELS
PLUS 2
FREE
MYSTERY GIFTS

HEARTSONG
PRESENTS

YES! Please send me 2 Free Heartsong Presents novels and my 2 FREE mystery gifts (gifts are worth about $10). After receiving them, if I don't wish to receive any more books I can return the shipping statement marked "cancel." If I don't cancel, I will receive 4 brand-new novels every month and be billed just $4.24 per book. That's a savings of 20% off the cover price. It's quite a bargain! Shipping and handling is just 50¢ per book in the U.S.* I understand that accepting the 2 free books and gifts places me under no obligation to buy anything. I can always return a shipment and cancel at any time. Even if I never buy another book, the two free books and gifts are mine to keep forever.

159 HDN FVYK

Name _____ (PLEASE PRINT) _____

Address _____ Apt. # _____

City _____ State _____ Zip _____

Signature (if under 18, a parent or guardian must sign)

Mail to the **Harlequin® Reader Service:**
IN U.S.A.: P.O. Box 1867, Buffalo, NY 14240-1867

* Terms and prices subject to change without notice. Prices do not include applicable taxes. Sales tax applicable in N.Y. This offer is limited to one order per household. Not valid for current subscribers to Heartsong Presents books. All orders subject to credit approval. Credit or debit balances in a customer's account(s) may be offset by any other outstanding balance owed by or to the customer. Please allow 4 to 6 weeks for delivery. Offer available while quantities last. Offer valid only in the U.S.

Your Privacy—The Harlequin® Reader Service is committed to protecting your privacy. Our Privacy Policy is available online at www.ReaderService.com or upon request from the Harlequin Reader Service.
We make a portion of our mailing list available to reputable third parties that offer products we believe may interest you. If you prefer that we not exchange your name with third parties, or if you wish to clarify or modify your communication preferences, please visit us at www.ReaderService.com/consumerschoice or write to us at Harlequin Reader Service Preference Service, P.O. Box 9062, Buffalo, NY 14269. Include your complete name and address.

REQUEST YOUR FREE BOOKS!

2 FREE INSPIRATIONAL NOVELS
PLUS 2
FREE
MYSTERY GIFTS

Love Inspired®

YES! Please send me 2 FREE Love Inspired® novels and my 2 FREE mystery gifts (gifts are worth about $10). After receiving them, if I don't wish to receive any more books, I can return the shipping statement marked "cancel." If I don't cancel, I will receive 6 brand-new novels every month and be billed just $4.49 per book in the U.S. or $4.99 per book in Canada. That's a savings of at least 22% off the cover price. It's quite a bargain! Shipping and handling is just 50¢ per book in the U.S. and 75¢ per book in Canada.* I understand that accepting the 2 free books and gifts places me under no obligation to buy anything. I can always return a shipment and cancel at any time. Even if I never buy another book, the two free books and gifts are mine to keep forever.

105/305 IDN FVYV

Name	(PLEASE PRINT)

Address	Apt. #

City	State/Prov.	Zip/Postal Code

Signature (if under 18, a parent or guardian must sign)

Mail to the Harlequin® Reader Service:
IN U.S.A.: P.O. Box 1867, Buffalo, NY 14240-1867
IN CANADA: P.O. Box 609, Fort Erie, Ontario L2A 5X3

**Are you a subscriber to Love Inspired books
and want to receive the larger-print edition?
Call 1-800-873-8635 or visit www.ReaderService.com.**

* Terms and prices subject to change without notice. Prices do not include applicable taxes. Sales tax applicable in N.Y. Canadian residents will be charged applicable taxes. Offer not valid in Quebec. This offer is limited to one order per household. Not valid for current subscribers to Love Inspired books. All orders subject to credit approval. Credit or debit balances in a customer's account(s) may be offset by any other outstanding balance owed by or to the customer. Please allow 4 to 6 weeks for delivery. Offer available while quantities last.

REQUEST YOUR FREE BOOKS!

2 FREE INSPIRATIONAL NOVELS
PLUS 2
FREE
MYSTERY GIFTS

Love Inspired

HISTORICAL
INSPIRATIONAL HISTORICAL ROMANCE

YES! Please send me 2 FREE Love Inspired® Historical novels and my 2 FREE mystery gifts (gifts are worth about $10). After receiving them, if I don't wish to receive any more books, I can return the shipping statement marked "cancel." If I don't cancel, I will receive 4 brand-new novels every month and be billed just $4.49 per book in the U.S. or $4.99 per book in Canada. That's a savings of at least 22% off the cover price. It's quite a bargain! Shipping and handling is just 50¢ per book in the U.S. and 75¢ per book in Canada.* I understand that accepting the 2 free books and gifts places me under no obligation to buy anything. I can always return a shipment and cancel at any time. Even if I never buy another book, the two free books and gifts are mine to keep forever.

102/302 IDN FV2V

Name	(PLEASE PRINT)

Address	Apt. #

City	State/Prov.	Zip/Postal Code

Signature (if under 18, a parent or guardian must sign)

Mail to the **Harlequin® Reader Service:**
IN U.S.A.: P.O. Box 1867, Buffalo, NY 14240-1867
IN CANADA: P.O. Box 609, Fort Erie, Ontario L2A 5X3

Want to try two free books from another series?
Call 1-800-873-8635 or visit www.ReaderService.com.

* Terms and prices subject to change without notice. Prices do not include applicable taxes. Sales tax applicable in N.Y. Canadian residents will be charged applicable taxes. Offer not valid in Quebec. This offer is limited to one order per household. Not valid for current subscribers to Love Inspired Historical books. All orders subject to credit approval. Credit or debit balances in a customer's account(s) may be offset by any other outstanding balance owed by or to the customer. Please allow 4 to 6 weeks for delivery. Offer available while quantities last.

Your Privacy—The Harlequin® Reader Service is committed to protecting your privacy. Our Privacy Policy is available online at www.ReaderService.com or upon request from the Harlequin Reader Service.

We make a portion of our mailing list available to reputable third parties that offer products we believe may interest you. If you prefer that we not exchange your name with third parties, or if you wish to clarify or modify your communication preferences, please visit us at www.ReaderService.com/consumerchoice or write to us at Harlequin Reader Service Preference Service, P.O. Box 9062, Buffalo, NY 14269. Include your complete name and address.

LIHDIR13

HEARTSONG

PRESENTS

Look out for 4 new
Heartsong Presents books next month!

**Every month 4 inspiring faith-filled
romances will be available in stores.**

These contemporary and historical Christian
romances emphasize God's role in every
relationship and reinforce the importance of
faith, hope and love.

LIHP48648

Jolie followed Morgan outside. There was a large gnarled oak tree still bent over as it had been all those years ago. She didn't stop until she reached it, turning his way only after they were beneath the wide expanse of limbs.

Morgan crossed his arms and studied the tree. "I remember having to climb up this tree and talk you down after you scrambled up to the top and froze."

She hadn't expected him to bring up old memories—it caught her a little off guard. "I remember how mad you were at having to rescue the silly little new girl."

A hint of a smile teased his lips, fraying Jolie's nerves at the edges. It had been a long time since she'd seen that smile.

"I got used to it, though," he said, his voice warming.

Electricity hummed between them as they stared at each other. Jolie sucked in a wobbly breath. Then the hardness in Morgan's tone matched the accusation in his eyes.

"What are you doing here, Jolie? Why aren't you taming rapids in some far-off place?"

"I…I'm—" She stumbled over her words. "I'm taking a leave from competition for a little while. I had a bad run in Virginia." She couldn't bring herself to say that she'd almost died. "Your dad offered me this teaching opportunity."

"I heard about the accident and I'm real sorry about that, Jolie," Morgan said. "But why come here after all this time?"

"This is my *home*."

Jolie saw anger in Morgan's eyes. Well, he had a right to it, and more than a right to point it straight at her.

But she'd thought she'd prepared for it.

She was wrong.

"Morgan," Jolie said, almost as a whisper. "I'd hoped we could forget the past and move forward."

Heart pounding, she reached across the space between them and placed her hand on his arm. It was just a touch, but the feeling of connecting with Morgan McDermott again after so much time rocked her straight to her core, and suddenly she wasn't so sure coming home had been the right thing to do after all.

*Will Morgan ever allow Jolie back into
his life—and his heart?*

Pick up HER UNFORGETTABLE COWBOY
from Love Inspired Books.

LIEXP0413RR

Will You Marry Me?

Bold widow Johanna Yoder stuns Roland Byler when she asks him to be her husband. To Johanna, it seems very sensible that they marry. She has two children, he has a son. Why shouldn't their families become one? But the widower has never forgotten his long-ago love for her; it was his foolish mistake that split them apart. This could be a fresh start for both of them—until she reveals she wants a marriage of convenience only. It's up to Roland to woo the stubborn Johanna and convince her to accept him as her groom in her home and in her heart.

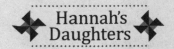

Johanna's Bridegroom
by
Emma Miller

Available May 2013

www.LoveInspiredBooks.com

LI8781